To
Terry,
with best wishes
for blue skies and
happy landings ahead!

Oran F. Remsnyder

Unforgettable Lady

A HISTORICAL FICTION NOVEL

BASED UPON REAL EVENTS

ORIN F. REMSNYDER

INFINITY
PUBLISHING

Copyright © 2005 by Orin F. Remsnyder

ISBN 0-7414-2710-9

Published by:

INFIN∞ITY
PUBLISHING.COM

1094 New DeHaven Street, Suite 100
West Conshohocken, PA 19428-2713
Info@buybooksontheweb.com
www.buybooksontheweb.com
Toll-free (877) BUY BOOK
Local Phone (610) 941-9999
Fax (610) 941-9959

Printed in the United States of America

Printed on Recycled Paper

Published August 2005

Dedication

This book is dedicated to the memory of my heroic brother Captain Don R. Remsnyder, a gallant jet fighter pilot, who gave his life in the service of the US Air Force during the Korean War.

And to all who served in the US Army Air Corps during World War II, especially to my 44-K cadet class buddies. And to the "Warbird" enthusiasts who keep vintage aircraft flying at air shows throughout the world.

One

New Guinea, 1945

The sunlit stillness of a tropic morning was shattered by the roar of a sleek, black, twin-engine fighter. The intensely focused, dark eyes of Sergeant Lou Fraley, the aircraft's ground crew chief, followed the plane's path as it began a steep climb to clear the mountain peak five miles beyond the west end of the Capur Airbase runway. Short of the summit, the plane banked sharply to the left and dove, flying low out over the bay, south of the airfield. Then the plane turned back toward the airstrip. Motionless, Fraley watched with concern as the plane flashed by, throttles wide open, barely ten feet above the steel-mesh landing strip.

Fraley was charged with the care of this aircraft and he "loaned" the plane to pilots to fly missions. This pilot, First Lieutenant Don Jennings, was engaging in a dangerous flight. As was his custom, Fraley had given the pilot a "thumbs up" signal as the plane started down the taxi strip. Now Fraley watched with alarm as the plane shot up like a rocket, as it again climbed steeply to avoid the five-thousand-foot peak dead ahead. As it neared the peak, the aircraft suddenly shuddered, and then hung in mid-air like a fluttering kite. Fraley winced as the craft plunged, tail first into the dense jungle below. The impact sent up a silent cloud of dust and debris.

"Good Christ! He bought the farm!" Fraley muttered. Turning on his heels, Fraley dashed for the radio shack, cursing with every step.

"Damn, dumb son-of-a-bitch! Stalled her in! Son-of-a-bitch!"

High up on the mountain, shaken and bruised, Jennings threw off his shoulder harness and unbuckled his seat belt. He turned to the gunner's seat, above and behind him, where Sergeant Jill Harris had been strapped in. She was slumped over; her head was against the gun sight, and a trickle of blood ran down her face. Jennings moved quickly to unfasten her safety belts. As he did so, Jill opened her eyes and whispered, "What happened?"

The moment Jill spoke Don realized he had fallen in love with her.

Their time together had been brief since a chance meeting just days ago. Jill had been working alone one evening when Don entered the office to inquire of flight schedules. In giving him a copy of the schedule, Jill had touched his hand lightly. Their eyes met and sparked a mutual attraction. Jill hadn't considered his rank, but only that his touch felt warm and good.

"Would you like to join me for a drink when you're finished here?" Don had boldly asked.

Don Jennings was handsome, five-ten, with broad shoulders, a boyish face and ash brown hair sticking out from under his unceremoniously perched cap. His warm smile displayed a perfect set of gleaming white teeth. A tinge of cockiness was evident in his low, masculine voice. Jill was impressed with his demeanor.

Without hesitating, Jill had taken him up on the invitation. But Jill's impulsive feelings were not without danger. Knowing enlisted personnel were never to fraternize with officers, she quickly suggested that they part separately. After Don told her where his quarters were located, she assured him that she would find him. He squeezed her hand gently, smiled and departed.

On her way to his quarters, Jill had second thoughts. Fearful that someone might see her enter his tent, she asked herself if this personal rendezvous would be worth the risk of losing her stripes or even her Army career. But Jill quickly put these thoughts aside—she had to know just what kind of man he was.

At the front of his tent, Jill hesitated briefly, and then knocked on the wooden screen door. Don beckoned her inside. He stood motionless, waiting for her to speak. Jill said nothing. Don broke the spell and reached for her hand. She took it and as their hands met, Don drew her to him. In an instant, her soft lips were pressing against his. Their embrace lasted for only a moment when Jill raised her arms and gently pushed him away. Looking up into his eyes, she whispered, "Hi there."

"Hi yourself young lady."

Slowly sitting down on his bed, they sat staring at each other.

"You know I shouldn't be here," she began.

"And why not?"

"I don't even know your name Lieutenant."

Touching her hand softly he said, "I'm Don Jennings. Who might you be?"

"Jill, Jill Harris. Sergeant Jill Harris. I'm temporarily assigned to flight operations, and I'm surprised we haven't met before."

"That's not surprising considering the number of pilots on this airfield, along with the shortage of airplanes."

"Well, I don't remember the names for the morning flights, so I don't know if you're scheduled to fly out tomorrow. Are you?"

"Yes, I have a flight to Weewak."

"May I ask where you're from?"

"Detroit," Jill proudly responded.

"You've got to be kidding! I lived there with my folks when Dad was at Selfridge Field, three years before I enlisted!"

"Well, small world isn't it?"

Don and Jill talked about the great auto capital; driving over the Ambassador Bridge; climbing the stairs of the tall Book Cadillac Building; and walking in River Rouge Park. They reminisced about their schools, home life, and family and friends that they had left behind.

Pausing briefly in their conversation, Don retrieved a bottle of blended whiskey from his footlocker. "I've kept this stashed away for some time, hoping for a special occasion."

"How lucky for me," Jill said with a coy smile.

One drink led to another and soon they were both feeling a warm glow. They sat their glasses on the floor and fell into a tight embrace, kissing passionately for several minutes before catching their breath. Then Jill abruptly pushed him away. "I guess we got a little carried away. It's getting late. I'm on duty early tomorrow, so I should get some sleep."

"Can we get together again soon?"

"I'd like that—if you think we can without getting into trouble."

"I'll be in touch with you as soon as I get back," he promised.

Don kissed Jill tenderly before she walked, quickly and on air, back to her quarters.

Since that first night together, Don and Jill had met secretly several more times. Jill had expressed an interest in flying with him, so Don decided to take her on his P-61 test flight. He had only meant to impress her with his daring maneuvers, but now Jill was sitting limply in the gunner's seat asking again, what had happened?

Jill moaned loudly as Don gently maneuvered and pulled her foot from its wedged position in the crumpled bulkhead. Carefully lifting her out of the seat, he carried her onto the wing and jumped the short distance to the ground. He carefully placed her on the soft grass and looked her over closely for injury. Other than the cut on her forehead and a badly bruised ankle, Jill seemed not to be severely hurt.

"Lie still until I find the others," Don commanded.

"Wait! I'll go with you."

"No way! Just stay put! You mustn't move just yet; I promise I'll be back soon."

"But I…" her voice trailed off.

A shout came from the rear of the wreckage. "Hey! Anybody home?" It was the unmistakable voice of his wisecracking radar operator, Lieutenant Jerry Hurwitz.

"Hey," Don yelled. "I'm com'n."

Hurwitz was sitting on the ground, leaning against the broken tail section. Blood streamed down his face from a wide gash on his scalp. When he saw his pilot leaning over him, Jerry smiled.

"That was one of the bumpiest landings I've ever had with you man!"

"Very funny! Now shut your trap and let me put something around that thick skull of yours. We have to stop that bleeding!" Ripping his shirt into strips, Don wrapped the makeshift bandage tightly around Jerry's head.

Motioning toward the rear of the plane Jerry said, "Tuskegee must be around here someplace."

A short distance away, Lieutenant Jordan "Tuskegee" Bond was trying to get to his feet. As Don approached the dazed airman, Bond asked, "What time is the next flight to Capur?"

"Geez, another joker in the group. Looks like we're all in one piece though," Don quickly added.

Guiding the two to Jill's motionless body, Don explained that she had slammed her head against the gun sight but that she seemed to be okay. Don covered her with his flight jacket, then informed them that he was heading back to the cockpit for the first aid kit.

Before Don returned, Jill had rallied. The foursome discussed their conditions, looked each other over, and concluded that, aside from Jerry's head wound, the injuries were certainly not life threatening.

Two hours had passed since the accident, but they had not seen even one search plane. They surmised that the base was unaware of the crash. Their radio was dead and there was no back-up equipment aboard. Then the sobering thought dawned on them that the mountain could be occupied by Japanese soldiers.

This mountain was treacherously steep—sloping sixty-five degrees at its peak. The thick canopy of ironwood trees and ferns would make it virtually impossible for an air rescue team to see them, and the use of their flare gun would give their position away to the enemy. As they mulled over their situation, the steaming jungle humidity became stifling, and flies and mosquitoes were beginning to swarm around them. The motley group sat looking at one another until Don stood up and addressed them as though commanding a garrison of troops.

"Listen," he began. "I got you in this mess, and now I'm going to get you out. Jerry isn't able to walk down this damn mountain. Jill, your ankle is too swollen to try it. Tuskegee can look after both of you until I get back with help."

"Wait a minute Don," Jerry argued. "We should stick together---we can carry Jill."

"He's right. We should all stay together," Jill insisted.

"Hold it! I can get down a lot faster alone. If I start now, I should be back by morning. Just be as quiet as you can, in case there are any Japs around up here."

The others realized it was useless to argue, and more or less bought into the idea that he was right. Don surveyed the scene. "Tuskegee," he began. "I'll need to borrow your shirt since I ripped mine apart to patch up Jerry. This shoulder holster could rub my skin raw in a hurry."

8

"Be my guest, buddy. Just be careful."

The three sat watching as Don put the shirt on and adjusted the shoulder holster. With the forty-five-caliber pistol secured inside the holster, he grabbed a canteen and a broad jungle knife from the plane's survival compartment. Then Don looked sympathetically at Jill. "You'll be okay. Stay quiet, rest and say a little prayer for me. I'll be back in no time."

Don felt a twinge of remorse, as if he was deserting them, but at the same time he knew he had to leave quickly—sensing their time was running out.

Don planted a soft kiss on Jill's forehead, shook hands with the two men, turned toward the south and disappeared into the dense jungle at the edge of the clearing.

"Don will make it. So let's just stay quiet and take it easy until he gets back," Jerry reassured them.

Tuskegee agreed, but Jill wasn't as confident. She felt uneasy and expressed a desire to move away from the downed plane, fearing that an enemy patrol might come upon them if they stayed right there beside the plane. "If there are Japs wandering around up here Lieutenant Hurwitz, wouldn't they easily spot this airplane?" She wanted to know.

"It's a chance we'll have to take. Besides that, it might make it harder for our guys to find us if we moved away from the plane. Don knows where we are," Jerry assured her.

"What if Don isn't with them?" Jill questioned.

"Jerry's right Jill. And even if Don isn't with the guys looking for us, he can give them directions to where we are," Jordan added.

Jill reluctantly agreed and dropped the subject. She tried to compose herself and hide her helpless feelings from her two male companions.

Two

ours had passed, and Don was losing sight of the sun as the afternoon tropical rain clouds formed. The jungle was turning very dark and Don's sense of direction was being affected. He stopped to compose himself, and as he stood, quietly, wiping his brow, he heard a strange hissing sound. At his feet, a coiled viper was about to strike, with its poisonous fangs targeting Don's left ankle! Jumping to the side, Don drew his pistol and fired, blowing the snake's head off. He kicked the dead varmint out of the way, and moved on cautiously.

With nightfall fast approaching, the air turned cold and damp. Don found a spot that seemed better than most, then cut several fronds and fashioned a bed and blanket. He shut his eyes and fell into a deep sleep.

At dawn streams of sunlight filtered through the jungle forest. The brisk morning air carried a soft sound of cascading water, a sound he had not identified before he collapsed into sleep the night before. Rising quickly, he followed the sound and shortly came upon the stream that flowed toward its plunge over a high precipice. Don thought that he had stopped at just the right time the evening before, as he could have stumbled into a bad situation in his weariness and in the low light of evening. He knelt beside the clear running stream, cupped his hands and vigorously splashed water on his arms and face. After refilling his canteen, he made his way downstream to the edge of the waterfall that dropped one hundred feet onto rocks below!

Don studied the terrain and finally decided that he could make his way down along side the falling waters where the jungle growth had feathered out. He would be careful and in no time he would put this obstacle behind him. And before he knew it he was safely over half way down and feeling confident. He started to think of how he would approach the air base and whom he would see first and what he would tell them.

Three quarters of the way down, as he visualized his triumphant return to base, his right foot wedged between two small rocks. Pulling free too abruptly, he lost his balance, fell backwards, careened end-over-end down the steep incline, and finally landed on his back on the jagged rocks below. He lay unconscious.

But, almost miraculously, his fall had not gone unnoticed. A young, dark-skinned native had witnessed Don's plunge.

One day ago, almost to the minute, the young native had been roaming near his village when he stopped to look toward the mountain peak five miles to the north. The clear morning, with no clouds in the sky revealed the high ground, a forbidden area, clothed in native superstition. Tribal legends told of evil spirits dwelling there. In addition, the tribal village had once been occupied by Japanese Army troops, until the Americans arrived and drove them out. The tribe feared the brutal Japanese soldiers and believed that remnants of Japanese troops still lurked high on the mountain.

This young tribesman, however, wanted to dispel the superstitions and to see for himself if the Japanese did inhabit the mountain. He had decided to explore the forbidden area, and in doing so, he believed his actions would serve as his right of passage from boyhood to manhood.

As the young native daydreamed, he heard the loud roar of a plane overhead. He watched as it headed for the mountain and recognized the white-star emblem on the wing as the marking of an American plane. He saw the plane nose upward toward the peak a second time. Just before reaching the top, the giant metal bird appeared to come to a full stop in the sky. Then it fell, disappearing into the jungle. An eerie silence filled the air. Dumb-founded, the young man stared in disbelief.

Rushing to his village to listen for talk of the crash, the lad found that many of the villagers were still asleep, and those that weren't were not aware of the crash. Now he believed he had another reason for climbing the mountain; he reasoned that helping Americans would be considered a good deed or— even heroic.

He filled a sack with dried food, beans and rice; topped his animal-hide canteen with water and placed a coat in his sack. Armed with his machete, the native hastily made his way toward the jungle highlands. He knew that working his way through the sharp, razor-like cuna grass to the foot of the mountain would be difficult at best. Aside from the heavy jungle underbrush, there could be poisonous snakes whose bite meant sudden death.

It took the rest of the day to reach the steep of the mountain. He felt a sense of accomplishment, as he explored the base of the mountain. Finally he decided to stop for the night near a towering waterfall, which he would climb in the morning, when he was rested.

When morning came he peered up at the waterfall and at the mountain peak behind it, and especially at the steep cliff that surrounded the falls. Even though he was an expert climber, he wondered what awaited him if he ventured the climb. He began a slow ascent alongside the cascading water. But as he started to climb, he looked up and saw the figure of a man falling backwards down the steep incline. The native for a moment was frozen with shock. "What was happening? Were there others around? Had the Japanese thrown someone over the cliff?" After a moment he realized there was no one else in the area, and he began moving towards the motionless body.

When the young native reached the unconscious man, he gently lifted him from the rocks and carried him a few feet to a small clearing. He placed a pillow of leaves under the man's head. The movement caused Don Jennings to awaken long enough to look into the bronzed, boyish face, then he lapsed into unconsciousness again.

Dipping some cool water from the falls, the rescuer bathed Don's blood-covered face. Don revived and slowly reached out his hand to touch the young native. With the young man's support, he tried to stand but a sharp pain struck him in his lower back and he fell to his knees gasping. Don motioned to the spot on his lower back. The tribesman understood and quickly fashioned a stretcher with jungle brush and two poles cut from small trees. Carefully placing him on the makeshift stretcher, the young native started the difficult drag down the slope.

After three bumpy hours of slow descent, they were down to the valley floor. Totally exhausted, the native stopped to rest. The young man took some food from his knapsack and offered it to his injured charge. Don stuffed the food into his mouth ravenously. Then they both sat staring at each other in silence knowing they had bonded without speaking. Don tried to stand again and found that the pain was not as bad as it had been hours before. After resting for a few minutes, they began their trek again, this time with Don leaning on the native.

After stumbling on for another half-hour, they stopped. The native was showing signs of weariness under Don's heavy weight. He offered Don a drink from the animal-hide canteen, and the water, although warm, was refreshing.

While resting, Don gazed at the young lad with brotherly affection. He wished he could converse with him like he had done so often with his older brother Tom. He wondered what his brother might be doing at this moment. The war had separated them. Tom had graduated from flight school one year before Don. The last he had heard from him was over two months ago when Tom was flying P-47 Thunderbolt fighters in Europe where he had shot down three enemy fighters. Don vividly remembered their boyhood days together that now seemed so long removed.

Don's most memorable years centered around their lives when they lived in Ohio. Their parents settled on a small farm ten miles from town. The boys were responsible for chores; chores that instilled within them a strong work ethic. In addition to working the family farm, they hired out to adjoining farmers whenever time permitted. They learned quickly to operate farm equipment and to do a man's work at an early age.

Even though Don was younger and shorter than Tom, their father showed no partiality. To make his point, he taught them how to defend themselves using skillful boxing techniques and often paired them off together in a three-round boxing match. Their mother disliked the practice immensely and refused to watch. Regardless, the lessons learned were not only for self-defense but taught Don and Tom how to be winners as well as good losers. Their Dad always knew when to stop the bouts before either boy lost control or was seriously hurt. Because of his shorter reach, Don had to get inside to land body blows. Unfortunately, he often felt the brunt of Tom's punches. Other times, however, he managed to land effective blows because of his strong determination and will to outwit his older brother. After each match, they shook hands and never ended a bout with any animosity.

Weak and barely able to stand, he vividly recalled these memories, and wondered what Tom would think if he knew of his present predicament. Don's personality lent itself to a lighter air than his brother's. He was the fun-loving, outgoing mischievous showman. Tom was more serious-minded and cautious. Don thought to himself...if he could have been more like his brother, he might have escaped this fate.

Don returned to reality and now thought about his immediate situation. They had reached the valley floor, and the pair had begun their way through the tall cuna grass. The sun bore down, and the humidity was stifling. Don grew weaker as he leaned heavily upon his young helper. Finally he sagged to the ground, too exhausted to go further. Don motioned for his friend to press on toward the air base. The tribesman gestured that he understood. Placing the canteen of water at Don's side, he disappeared into the tall cuna grass in the direction of the airfield.

Back at the base, in the meantime, Sgt. Fraley had rushed to flight headquarters to report the accident to squadron commander Colonel Bates. But Bates had flown to Weewak Island and Major Richards was in charge, so Fraley told the Major what he had seen and then volunteered to head up a search and rescue team. To Fraley's dismay, Richards was reluctant to authorize the search until Colonel Bates returned. Fraley left operations in disgust; he was determined to get help for the downed crew.

Noticing a group of men standing outside the mess hall, he approached them. "Fellas," he began, "we've got an airplane down and no one at headquarters is willing to authorize a search party. There were three men and a female on board, my pilot Lt. Don Jennings, his OR Lt. Hurwitz and two observers—Sgt. Jill Harris and transport pilot Lt. Bond. Major Richards wants us to wait 'till Colonel Bates gets back to base. I aim to start out in an hour, even if I have to go by myself. I may get court-martialed, but I'm going. Any of you willing to help?"

"Hell, Lou, you know that crew must be dead after hitting that mountain," interjected Mitch Shafer, a fellow crew chief. "All we'll be doing is bringing back bodies and that's a job for grave registration," Mitch added.

"What about the Japs up in those hills?" one of the men retorted. "We'd be sitting ducks!"

"Bullshit," yelled Lieutenant Jake Keaton. "We owe it to them, Japs or no Japs. I say we do what is needed. If there is no rescue by tomorrow morning, we need to get our asses in gear and go up that mountain with or without orders to do so!"

Keaton was an officer and a popular pilot in the squadron, and he was a good friend of Don Jennings and Jerry Hurwitz. Keaton's remarks instantly motivated twenty men to join in the search. Lou and Keaton suggested knapsacks with C-rations, rifles, side arms, machetes and stretchers. In less than half an hour, the pumped up rescue squad was ready to make their way toward the mountain. They agreed to leave in 24 hours if no official rescue mission was organized before then.

Running like an antelope, the young tribes-man approached the north side of the unfenced and relatively deserted base around one o'clock in the afternoon. He came upon a tent with a large red cross painted on the door. He stood there, wondering what he should do, when suddenly the door opened and an Army nurse came out. She was initially startled by his gestures but quickly realized the urgency in his motions. At that moment, Lt. Keaton came upon the scene, on his way to gather the renegade rescue team. Both Keaton and the nurse tried in vain to make sense of the young man's chatter.

Unable to understand the exhausted young man, Keaton suggested they seek out Bengi, a local native, who worked with the base cook. Keaton guided the boy to the mess hall where he was given food and water. Bengi understood the boy's dialect and learned why he had come to the base. His story led Keaton to suspect the injured man was likely one of the crewmen of the downed aircraft.

Bengi told Keaton that the young native wanted to lead them to the man.

Fraley and the rest of the search team had already assembled and were awaiting Keaton's arrival. The team headed out following the young native. And within an hour they came upon Don, laying face down on the grass. Rolling him over, Keaton was relieved to see that Don had just been sleeping. Once aroused, Jennings looked up into their faces with gratitude.

Keaton asked if the others had survived. In a weak voice, Don replied, "Yes, all of them. They're straight north of the waterfalls, probably six miles from here."

Keaton turned to look for the young native who had led them. He was gone.

Two of the men carried Jennings back to the base hospital on a stretcher. The others formed behind Keaton and Fraley to begin their trek toward the steep slopes.

Meanwhile, a scouting patrol of six Japanese infantrymen had been searching the mountain for several hours trying to locate the American plane. At one point, they were only a half-mile from the wreckage. Two of the patrol had been even closer, but were too far west on the mountain slope. They reversed their course and now were headed east toward the center of the mountain, assuring the survivors' salvation for the moment.

At one point Jerry thought he heard voices; voices too quick and sharp in tone to be American. So Jerry, Jordan and Jill were sweating it out and getting more apprehensive by the moment about Don's success in reaching the air base. It was now noon of the second day since the crash and he had not returned. Attempting to hide his concern, Jerry told jokes, quietly, and poked fun at the military. Jill and Jordan pretended to be amused. Every hour or so, Jill dressed Jerry's wound with iodine, much to his displeasure. Nevertheless the treatments thus far had prevented infection.

Although the trio hadn't known each other before the flight, they now had developed a close comradeship. The men were especially concerned about Jill's safety. As the hours passed, their anxiety escalated.

"Why is Don taking so long?" Jill complained.

"Well, suppose it were any one of us trying to work our way down this damn mountain. Give him a little more time and we'll be hearing from someone soon," Jerry said reassuringly.

"Look, Jerry, you're the only one who really knows Don Jennings. You've flown with him for months. Neither Jill nor I know a damn thing about this guy, except he managed to put this airplane down gently enough for us to walk away in one piece," Jordan remarked.

Jill remained silent.

"Yes, I've been with him for over a year. We met at Fresno, California, where I was assigned to train with him. Don and I have been as close as any two men could be. In fact I was best man at his wedding. Let me tell you that Don is one of the best pilots in this squadron. Whatever happened up there yesterday was not his fault. The guy's a natural flyer and knows this airplane inside out. He's flown P-61's for over a year and a half and has mastered this type of aircraft, if anyone has. As far as him getting back to the base, I'd stake my life on it. He's probably there right now getting together a rescue team."

Jill, listening intently, was stunned to learn that Don had a wife. She hid her emotions that were erupting after that karate chop to the throat. Inside, she felt as though her heart would break. Jerry sensed instantly he had blurted out the wrong thing. He knew Don was sweet on Jill and had enticed her to come along on this flight. Jerry hoped his slip-of-the-lip would not jeopardize Jill's friendship with Don.

Now night was upon them once again. They fell silent and huddled together to keep warm.

In the silence, Jill's mind was plagued by Jerry's disclosure. Don had not leveled with her and she had fallen in love with him. As she lay there trying to fall asleep, tormenting questions surfaced. "Why hadn't he told her the truth? Did he really love her or was he still in love with his wife? What is going to happen if she does get off this mountain? Could she face him now?"

Three

*J*ordan Bond had fallen asleep after the conversation about Don Jennings. He was awakened by a cramp in his leg; a leg that had been weighted down by Jill's body when she rolled over. Jordan massaged his leg and tried to go back to sleep. But sleep was past, as Jordan's thoughts had turned to his sorry predicament. He wondered why he had allowed Don Jennings to persuade him to come along on this ill-fated flight. But as soon as he had asked himself the question, he knew the answer; Jennings and Hurwitz were the only flyers on Capur who hadn't treated him like Jim Crow.

Jordan had returned from Europe as the war there wound down. He had served with the

"Tuskegee Airmen" in the 99th Pursuit Squadron—
the only "Negro Pilot Squadron" in the Army Air
Corps. After finishing his tour, Jordan was sent back
to the States and assigned to ground duty, as the Air
Force had no more need for single-engine fighter
pilots for the South Pacific Theater of Operations.
Jordan wanted his freedom in the air; he wanted to
fly again. So he transferred to the Air Transport
Command, and learned to fly multi-engine aircraft.
Soon he was flying transport planes to bases in the
South Pacific.

The Army still held to their segregation
policy, and when Jordan arrived at Capur, he was
given separate quarters from the white airmen.
White officers ignored him and enlisted personnel
refused to salute him.

Then, several days ago, as he stood alone
outside the base officer's club, Jordan was
approached by Lieutenants Don Jennings and Jerry
Hurwitz.

Never having seen a black officer, the two
airmen were intrigued at the sight of Jordan, and
they were captivated when they noticed silver pilot
wings emblazoned on his jacket. Jordan was
surprised that the white officers talked to him, and
more so when they invited him to join them in the
club. Though there were no Whites Only signs,
Jordan had before been too reluctant to enter. Now
he felt compelled to accept their invitation, and
confident that his presence would be accepted, as he
timidly followed them inside. Four drinks later,
most of Jordan's tensions had dissipated and Don

and Jerry were calling their new friend, "Tuskegee." When Jordan learned that Don and Jerry were the crewmen of the P-61 Black Widow, he was anxious to learn more about the huge fighter. Then he was elated when Don invited him to fly with them the following morning.

Now, however, Jordan wondered if it had been worth it. Was his extra weight a factor in the accident? As he pondered such negative thoughts, he gazed at the radar compartment where he and Jerry had been seated before the crash. As the dawn brightened, Jerry awakened to see Jordan staring at the fuselage.

"Can't sleep, Tuskegee?" Jerry asked.

"I slept some. Been thinkin' about this airplane."

"What about it?"

"She's an awesome looking bird."

"Yeah. Not too many of 'em exist, and almost none have made it out here yet. This is the first one we've had in our squadron. We're supposed to get more when they arrive at Biak."

"I heard about them in Europe but never saw one. It's the only military plane painted glossy black…I've been told," Jordan replied.

"Makes 'em almost invisible by search lights. Northrop specifically designed it for use against German bombers attacking Britain at night. Because of its color and firepower they named it the "Black Widow."

"I really didn't have a chance to learn much about this bird on our flight, since you guys squeezed me into your little radar compartment," Jordan jokingly complained.

"Anything ya wanna know, just ask me," Jerry offered.

"Is this the latest design model?" Jordan asked.

"Yep. It's a "C" model. We were trained in the "B" but this has more firepower. This baby has four fifties and a twenty millimeter cannon; air brakes on the top and bottom of the wings to slow our air speed whenever we need and we can turn on a dime."

"What's her cruise?"

"We cruise at three thirty, but she'll top out at four-hundred and thirty miles per hour," Jerry bragged.

Jerry's enthusiastic description prompted Jordan to continue his query, and Jerry appeared to feel better as he talked.

"What's her range?" Jordan pressed.

"Over seventeen hundred miles."

"Largest fighter I've ever seen," Jordan admitted.

"They don't make 'em any bigger," Jerry proudly stressed.

"Now that I'm multi-rated, maybe when we get out of this mess and I get back to the States again, I could try to transition into one of these Widows," Jordan said, only half-joking.

"No tell'n how long this war out here is gonna last, but I've heard we'll soon be head'in for the Lengayen Gulf as soon as our squadron gets a full compliment of P-61's," Jerry confided.

As Jordan and Jerry chatted, Jill slumbered....passing another long night, patiently awaiting whatever was to come. The security Jill felt while Jordan was beside her had disappeared when he moved to stretch his legs, and now the pain in Jill's ankle awakened her. She reached down to rub it and found that her left ankle was twice the size of her right. She knew she couldn't put weight on it. A ridiculous thought crossed her mind. "I should find some ice to put on the swelling." Then she quietly laughed at herself as she excused the thought.

Unlike the three men who accompanied her on this flight, Jill Harris was a non-commissioned enlistee. She had joined the Women's Army Auxiliary Corps six months ago. Jill felt and acted much older than her twenty years. Her quick rise in rank to sergeant was due to her intelligence, her hard-working spirit and her leadership ability, which was quickly recognized by her superiors. Growing up, Jill had moved about the world with her parents and had spent time in the Philippines as a child. She had learned the language, Filipino, and was bilingual at the age of seven. When her father was stationed at Selfridge Field, near Detroit, Jill was a teenager, and the United States was at war in the South Pacific. Since along the way she had also learned the Japanese language in Hawaii, Jill decided to enlist as an interpreter in the Army.

Jill was five-foot four inches tall and beautifully proportioned, with dark skin, hair and eyes. She could easily pass as a Philippino. She knew she was attractive but never flaunted her looks. She was often the target of men's advances, not only by enlisted men but by the officers as well. She seemed to have much more in common with the officers, but since enlisted personnel were not to fraternize with commissioned officers, she did not date. The other women in the squadron liked her open, supportive ways. Inwardly, Jill longed to have a relationship with a mature man, preferably a pilot just like her own father. This desire was suppressed until two weeks ago when she met First Lieutenant Don Jennings.

Now, two weeks later, here she sat, on the ground, in a jungle, lost somewhere on a God-forsaken mountain filled with enemy soldiers and poisonous snakes, and she was unable to walk and fearing for her life. As she looked at the giant plane beside her, stuffed into its strange leafy vine nest, Jill was impressed with how little damage it had suffered. She imagined that if a runway were available, the plane could be flown right off its perch, provided it could be hoisted onto its landing gear and rigged with new props.

Her mind was shoring up her faith—now she was convinced that help was coming. Good things had happened so quickly these last two weeks, certainly there would be more good to come—a happy ending to this horrible trial. Until the crash, every moment had held increasing excitement and anticipation, culminating in the invitation to experience a flight in the huge P-61 Black Widow night fighter, with Don Jennings at the controls.

Even though she had known him only a matter of days, Don had become her "knight in shinning armor." But now she constantly worried about the gunshot they had heard shortly after Don had started down the mountain. And the shining armor…was that the glossy black fuselage of a Black Widow airplane? Of course it was, and the Widow, who would be the widow? Until yesterday Jill hadn't had a clue that Don had a wife back in the States, and each time that thought surfaced, her heart cried inside her. Jill couldn't bare the thought that Don had been killed by the enemy. It was worse than the thought of her fate if Don was now dead.

Four

Squadron Commander Colonel Joe Bates had flown to Biak Island to find out if any new P-61's were available for his fighter pilots at Capur. None had arrived. When he returned and received the news of the loss of his only P-61, he was furious. He was also notified of the search party and the return of the downed aircraft's pilot. He headed for the base hospital fully expecting the worst. He was surprised to find Lt. Don Jennings, his best trained pilot, conscious and talking with a staff doctor.

When Bates appeared, Don knew judgment day was at hand. "Well," Bates began. "Looks as though you managed to walk away from a bad one. How are you Lieutenant?"

"To tell you the truth Colonel, I feel as though my back is broken." One of the doctors standing nearby informed Bates that x-ray results would be forthcoming.

"Lt. Jennings, what about Lt. Hurwitz?"

"I'm afraid he was the most seriously injured Sir. And there are two others with him up there."

"What?" Bates retorted. "You mean you had three people with you?"

"Yes Sir. In addition to Jerry, Jordan Bond, a transport pilot and Sgt. Jill Harris went along as observers to look for Japanese troops on the mountain."

"How the hell did you get four people aboard a three-capacity crew aircraft?" Bates snapped.

"Well Sir, I had Lt. Bond aft with Jerry in the radar seat position and Sgt. Harris was sitting in the gun turret seat."

Col. Bates stood beside the bed rubbing his chin slowly. Speaking softly, Bates asked about the injuries.

"Jerry has a deep scalp wound, but I think he should heal okay. Sgt. Harris has a badly bruised left ankle. Lt. Bond has only some minor cuts and bruises. I left him behind to look after the others till I could get back with help."

An orderly approached with two x-rays and handed them to the attending physician. After reviewing the films, for only two minutes or less, the doctor approached Don.

"Young man, you have several fractured vertebrae. For that to heal, you will have to have

34

your lower back immobilized. I am ordering a full body cast. It won't be fun, but it will allow you to fully mend in about eight weeks. And if all goes well, it may turn out that you will be good as new."

Col. Bates was asked to leave so that the body cast procedure could be done immediately. Bates left to find the crew who had delivered Don on the stretcher. They told Bates of the Dani tribesman who had brought Jennings down the mountain, and about the makeshift rescue team. The Commander was troubled by the news of Lt. Keaton and Sgt. Fraley's unauthorized search and rescue mission.

After his talk with the men, Bates thought about what to do next. Because of the two unauthorized personnel aboard the plane, some disciplinary action would have to be taken against Jennings. Bates was not one to make rash decisions without knowing all the facts, but he was duty-bound not only to keep his pilots and crews as sharp as possible, but especially to ensure that they operated within regulations. He had told his pilots on more than one occasion that there was no room for "fuck-ups" in his command. He knew Don Jennings well and considered him a "hot" pilot who did not seem to be reckless, although Bates was aware of Don's cockiness at times. He decided to reserve judgment pending further review and investigation of details about the accident.

At that moment, roughly four and a half miles away, Keaton, Fraley and their rescue team had negotiated the steep climb and were now above the waterfall, heading due north. It was getting dark.

They would have to wait till morning to continue the search. Fraley suggested they fire a flare to see if they could get a response from any survivors. Keaton was reluctant and fearful it would alert possible enemy patrols. Fraley persisted, believing they were close to the crash site. He felt the downed crew could respond by shooting a flare to pinpoint their location. Fraley won out and a flare was sent up.

Jill was the first to see the red flare pierce the night sky, and excitedly she pointed it out to the others. Although all three were ecstatic, the moment was short-lived. Jerry posed some pertinent questions. Was this a trick of the Japanese, to get the crew to give away their location by returning a distress flare? Or, was this truly an American rescue party trying to find them?

"It must be our guys," shouted Bond.

"Like hell it is, it's a trick!" Jerry insisted.

"Nonsense," Jill added. "If they are this close, no matter if they are friendly or not, they will spot us soon anyway. I say we respond."

They fell silent, all thinking the unavoidable thoughts...of the horrific stories of cruelty inflicted by the Japanese on their prisoners, and the nightmares they each had had about being captured. They'd wait till morning.

"Why the hell don't they respond?" Fraley snapped.

"Probably afraid to, for fear of the Japs," Lt. Keaton replied. They elected to wait until daylight to continue their search.

Jordan had dozed off and was snoring loudly, as Jill's mind raced on. Why hadn't Don leveled with her? One moment she hated Don for lying to her and the next moment tears rolled down her cheeks as she wished she were in his arms. This dilemma with Don was not her only concern. She couldn't help thinking that this accident could damage her future in the Army. She knew all accidents were investigated. She would have to tell her side of the story. How would this affect her career? She wished she could stop thinking about it and go to sleep. She prayed for the break of day.

As dawn broke, Keaton awakened the men and told them to chow down quickly and prepare to move out. Lou Fraley had already eaten and was anxious to get started. In no time the group was on the move again.

An hour passed and they stopped to rest. Lou decided to call out to see if he could get a response. His first shout was heard by Jill. Jerry and Jordan were still half dozing. Nudging Jerry, she cried out, "I just heard someone yelling. Listen, there's a voice calling from down below!" Jerry quickly poked Jordan. All three strained to hear more sounds in the morning air.

"Hello, Americans. Can anyone hear me? Hello," the voice of Lou Fraley came through clearly.

Bond shouted, "Yo, we're up here!"

Further down the slope, the rescue team heard the faint response and they quickened their steps. Within ten minutes, Lou broke through the clearing that the aircraft had cut in its fall. There before him, fifty yards away, lay the wreckage, and the threesome huddled beside the wing. He dashed toward Lt. Hurwitz. Jerry held out his hand and Lou grabbed it. Tears welled up in both their eyes.

Lt. Keaton directed the medics to check the injuries of Lt. Hurwitz and Sgt. Harris; the colored guy could wait. The radio operator was instructed to break radio silence and contact the base headquarters to report of their success.

Colonel Bates received the message that the search team had located the aircraft and that they were bringing down the injured crew. Bates decided to talk again with Lt. Jennings. He knew that a broken back required intense medical attention, attention that this small base could not provide. Jennings would soon be sent back to the States to recuperate.

At the hospital, which was little more than a MASH unit, Bates found Don encased in a full body cast. Don greeted the Colonel with a smile and extended his hand of welcome instead of a salute. Bates found it difficult not to be sympathetic. He liked Jennings, not only because he was his best pilot, but also because Jennings had rescued him from a close call during transitional training back in the States, just before they had rotated overseas. Nevertheless, Bates had to get to the bottom of the cause of this crash. A detailed report was required for his superiors. Totaling a $170,000 P-61 Black Widow night fighter, grounding its pilot permanently and causing injuries to three others, would not be taken lightly, especially since all consequences were not combat-related and the flight was unauthorized.

Bates proceeded. "Lieutenant, what was the purpose of that flight?"

"Colonel, you know I've waited a long time to get an airplane so I could engage in the fight out here. I needed to check out this new bird you had assigned me to see how she handled before going on my first mission. So I took her for a test flight. I guess my official answer would be that I thought a test flight was needed—was required."

"Didn't you think I would give you a check-out before sending you on a mission?"

"Well you may have if time permitted, Sir, but you were away, time was available, and who knows what urgent situation would be at hand by the time you returned, or even before you returned. I thought I should be prepared if and when that first call came."

"So what caused you to fly into that mountain peak?"

"That's what I don't understand Colonel. I was about to clear the peak when suddenly the plane shuddered, lost lift and was about to drop off to the left in a stall. When I realized what was happening, I did the only thing I could do. I cut the switches and ruddered her down to avoid going in nose first."

"Couldn't you feel that stall coming?" Bates queried.

"No, as a matter of fact, I couldn't. That's a first for me in a P-61, and you know I've logged over a thousand hours in 61's since I started flying them a year ago. Colonel, the air speed indicator must have given me a false reading because the needle never approached the stall marker on the dial."

"Okay, let's let it go at that. I hope you can sell that story to the accident review board. The group commander of this Fifteenth Air Force isn't going to be happy about losing this airplane, not to mention your injury and those of the others."

When Bates left, Don felt as though he had left his commander down. Did Bates believe his account of the faulty instrument reading? If not, how was this going to affect the board's findings? God, what was I thinking when I pulled a damn stunt like that?

Then, for the first time since the accident, Don's mind turned to home and his wife Betty. Don loved Betty and he had never been unfaithful to her until he met Jill. What will this do to Betty and to their marriage? Don would have plenty of time now to reflect and rearrange his priorities. He was beginning to realize that his life had changed drastically, and may never again be what he had always thought it was and would be. With the real possibility of not having a flying career in the military, what did he have left?

Five

As Don Jennings looked back on his first meeting with Betty, he had fond memories. Don remembered his initial weekend leave, after arriving at the airfield to begin his pilot training. While leisurely strolling down the main street in the small town near the airfield, he noticed a very pretty, young brunette pumping gasoline at a street-side service station. She was focused on her work and hadn't noticed him walking toward her. Presently, a man came out of the station and handed her some bills. She gave him his change, the man tipped his hat, got into his car and drove away. Don walked boldly up to her. "Good afternoon Miss. My name is Don Jennings.

I'm stationed at the airfield and this is my first time in town."

"How can I help you?"

"Looks like you work here, so I thought maybe you'd tell me what a guy could do around here on a Saturday night?"

"Yes, I do work here, and in answer to your question, you can take a hike," she replied sarcastically.

"Well, I'm a long way from home and I was wishing you might consider showing me around town."

"You certainly get right to the point, Mister."

"Oh, you know how to address cadets I see," Don quipped.

"I recognize your uniform. I know that's what they call pilot trainees at the base because I've gone to a few of the dances there with my USO group."

Don knew she was warming up to him. "I wish you would have dinner with me 'cause I don't know a soul in this town," he continued.

Looking him over from head to toe, she smiled and in a soft voice said, "Well, I had promised to go to the movies with my girlfriend tonight. I guess I can cancel. What time could you come by?"

Don's heart skipped a beat as he blurted out, "Whenever you say. I've nothing to do the rest of the afternoon."

"I'm used to eating by 5:30, if that's okay."

"Great! But wait, where do you live?"

"See that street over there? That's Juniata Street. I live down that street in the second block, number 203. It's a tan stucco Spanish-style house. You can't miss it. Now I must get back to work since I have some inside duties to finish before I leave."

"Now seriously, you won't stand me up will you?"

"Of course not, silly. I'm not that kind of girl. Besides, I think it would be fun," she added with a smile.

"Hey, you haven't told me your name."

"It's Betty...Betty Marsh," she said laughingly.

"Well, Miss Betty Marsh, I'll look forward to seeing you at 5:30 sharp."

"I'll be ready Mister Jennings," she said as she waved and walked inside the station.

Don was elated that she agreed to go out with him. Little did he know that Betty Marsh hadn't had a date in weeks. Aside from serving in the USO group, she had done nothing but work since she graduated from high school. She was awaiting acceptance into nursing school. Her male school chums were all in the service, and she had avoided dating service men at the local training base because they were always on the move. Don Jennings, however, touched a warm spot in her heart when he spoke to her so innocently.

Their first date went better than either could have imagined, and it led to many more, as the two became completely and hopelessly infatuated with each other. The courtship blossomed into a serious, romantic love affair, which played out like clockwork on Wednesdays and weekends as a result of Don's training schedule. After logging thirty-five hours of solo time, Don became an upper classman and was granted leave on Wednesday nights as well as on weekends, and every moment of his free time was devoted to Betty during this most wonderful time in his life.

Don's daydream finally floated away, and he was again left with his current reality. He felt a thousand sticky itches as he lay there alone in his body cast. Forced to make friends with himself in his solitary plaster cell, eventually he could not avoid confronting uncomfortable inner thoughts. Don realized that perhaps it was his hedonistic attitude had led to his brief relationship with Jill Harris. With time to think about what he had done, Don had difficulty rationalizing his unfaithfulness to Betty. His combat tour would end with his evacuation back to the States; therefore there would be no further close contact with Jill. Regardless, he had deep feelings for her and was very concerned for Jill's safety.

Don's thoughts again focused on Betty and memories of their good times. They had shared so much before his departure for the war zone. Little things came to mind---like the day she surprised him with a birthday cake. She baked his favorite yellow cake with chocolate icing, topping it with nineteen candles. He loved to hear her play the piano and watch her sketch. He admired the way she carried herself. To him, she was not only pretty, but she possessed a heart of compassion and love. The little things—maybe they weren't so little after all—maybe they were what it was all about—what he was in the war to fight for—what had become, or should have become, the central purpose of his life.

After he graduated from primary flight school, his country club lifestyle at Ryan Aeronautical School in the small apricot-grove-laden little town of Hemet came to an end. His dreamy days of open cockpit flying in the Stearman PT-17 also ended. He had finished his initial phase of flight training. And while he would move on to a sleeker, faster, fighter-type aircraft, he was saddened to leave. He had danced with clouds on warm summer days and romanced with Betty on his free hours off base. Now he would no longer be near her. He had to move on to a new phase of flight training.

He boarded a troop train for "who knows where?" The train transported him and the other cadets to a siding in Needles, Arizona where they sat overnight. In the morning the train rumbled across the Mojave Desert in 110-degree heat, winding up at Gardner Field near Taft in the San Joaquin Valley, 120 miles north of Los Angeles.

The airfield location was a far cry from the paradise of Hemet. At first Don hated the place. It was purgatory, with a whiff of petroleum up his nose and heaping doses of dust in his mouth. Despite the churning sound of oil derricks, dust and heat, Don looked back fondly on Gardner Field as the place where he became not just a man, but a polished pilot as well. Furthermore, the base's proximity to Hollywood afforded him an opportunity to weekend visits at the Hollywood canteen. There, movie stars waited on the GIs who came for coffee and doughnuts and a chance to dance with the likes of Doris Day, Bette Davis, Francis Langford and Rita Hayworth. Tragedy and the hectic flight training at Gardner Field also filled Don's memories of the times away from Betty.

During this phase of training, Don was flying an all-metal, low-wing basic trainer, the BT-13. The trainer was nicknamed the "Vultee Vibrator" due to the loud noises it made when the pitch of the propeller was changed during flight. Pilots who flew the plane joked about this characteristic but liked its performance and handling qualities. This airplane was a big change from the slower, open cockpit primary trainer he was used to. With its four hundred and fifty horse-powered engine and a sliding canopy over the tandem cockpits, the plane resembled a fighter aircraft. On the other hand, the aircraft's spin characteristics presented a new danger. The inability to recover control after a three-turn spin in the ship usually had tragic results.

The fledgling cadet pilots were required to do more aerobatics, tight formation, cross-country, night and instrument flying.

As Don reflected on these times, he remembered how concerned Betty had become when she learned of a mid-air crash involving two military aircraft at his base. Don believed that if she were told the whole story of what had happened to him that tragic day, her fears for his safety would have greatly magnified.

The fact that he was scheduled to be in one of the aircraft involved in the crash that very day was a chilling experience for Don. As was the drill each morning, one of three cadet pilots was to leave with the flight instructor; fly for an hour, then land at a designated auxiliary field. There the instructor's other two cadets would be waiting for their turn to go up with their instructors. On the day of the accident, Don awoke early with a throbbing toothache. He asked his roommate, Cadet Ron Taylor, to take his place in the early morning flight schedule. Taylor was to inform their instructor, Lieutenant Ginter, that Don had gone on sick call.

After seeing the dentist, Don caught the military bus to the auxiliary field where Lt. Ginter and Cadet Taylor would land upon completing the training flight.

Don arrived at the auxiliary field just as the first flights of the morning were landing. Two of the training planes did not show up. One of them was Lieutenant Ginter's aircraft.

After an hour's wait, an AT-6 (Advanced Trainer), landed at the field. A young flying officer climbed out of the plane and dashed into the ready room where Don and another cadet were waiting patiently for their instructors to arrive. After a brief telephone conversation, the young flying officer hung up and turned to the two cadets.

"Are you two waiting for your instructors?"

"I am, Sir," Don answered.

"Me too, Sir," the other cadet said.

"I'm afraid your planes will not be coming in. You'd both better catch the bus back to your quarters and wait for further orders," he said sadly.

When he arrived back at his barracks, Don found that all that remained on his roommate's area of their shared cubical was an empty, bare-spring, bunk. As he stood staring at the bunk, he was approached by the Commandant of Cadets who ordered him to report immediately to the flight line.

Obeying the order, Don hurried to the operation's office in hopes of seeing Cadet Taylor and Lt. Ginter. Instead, he was met by a stern-looking officer who introduced himself as flight instructor, Lieutenant King.

Unsympathetically, King informed Don that his instructor had been killed in a mid-air collision along with another pilot and two cadets.

"I've been assigned Lieutenant Ginter's cadets. You were scheduled for a flight lesson today Mister Jennings. Get your chute and let's go for a ride," Lt. King commanded.

Stunned after this news, Don hesitated for a moment, then turned away and headed out to retrieve his parachute as Lt. King had directed. Images of his last moments with his buddy, Cadet Taylor, flashed in his mind as he walked. "Taylor and Lt. Ginter dead?" Don couldn't conceive of it, yet he had seen Taylor's bunk stripped to the bare springs!

"Jesus, it must be true," he told himself.

"And this officer King...what kind of calloused bastard is he?" Don wondered.

Don put on his chute and moved quickly toward the plane. He climbed up on the wing and flung himself into the front cockpit. King was already seated at the rear.

As soon as Don turned on his intercom, he heard the order to take off and climb to five thousand feet. King's voice came over the intercom with new instructions. "We're gonna do some power off stalls, Jennings. Then I want you to give me a two-turn spin to the left."

"Roger, Sir," Don acknowledged.

Don did a three hundred and sixty degree banking turn to clear the area below him as he had been trained to do before pulling up into a stall or going into a spin. When he had completed the maneuvers, King was on the intercom again.

"Someone this morning failed to do what you just did Mister. That's why those pilots were killed today. One of those pilots didn't clear himself above and below before he started his maneuvers. Don't ever forget that Jennings," King shouted. "Okay, Mister, take us back to the field, that's enough for today," Lt. King added coldly.

When they landed, Don was dismissed. As he walked slowly back to his quarters, Don, for the first time, realized it could have been him in that fatal accident instead of Cadet Taylor! Young Don Jennings believed then, as he did now, that fate was playing a hand in his life.

Six

Upon completing his basic flight training, Don was ordered to Texas in early spring for advanced flight training. Eagle Air Force Base was larger than Don's previous field, and it was specifically designed for handling twin-engine trainers. Located in the dry, isolated plains of west Texas, the geography offered ideal flying weather, most of the time. A prevailing westerly wind made the traffic pattern simple. But, occasionally an intense northerly crosswind would sweep in and create tricky landing conditions and dangerous challenges for students.

Flying cadets were introduced to the Cessna UC-78, better known as the "Bamboo Bomber." Built strictly for twin-engine instructional purposes, its two-place, side-by-side cockpit had dual controls and instrument panels, flanked by two 245-horsepower engines mounted on fabric-covered low wings. Gangly landing gear allowed the lightweight craft to wobble when it sat on the ground with engines running. Although reliable, the ungainly looking "Witchita Wobbler" was the brunt of many a joke by cadets.

Don's instructor was First Lieutenant J.D. Stine, a combat veteran from the European Theater who had distinguished himself as a B-25 bomber pilot. Don felt fortunate to have the opportunity to learn from such a seasoned pilot, and he set out to learn every skill he could from Stine, whose reputation was one of toughness and perfection. Don immediately wondered why the man was so particular about every aspect of flying. Before long Don would discover at least one reason for himself.

The final advanced flight training was sixteen weeks. Don was intensely focused on mastering the twin-engine trainer, and he soon became highly proficient at the controls. A cock-sure attitude was forming within him as he neared his status of a commissioned pilot officer.

Then, on one of his night cross-country flights, he learned why Lt. Stine was such a strict disciplinarian. On a "buddy flight," such as this one, Don flew with Cadet Pete Allen as his co-pilot. The flight plan called for them to fly east to Sonora, south to Del Rio and then return to their base. This triangular course was part of the final stages of training. The first leg was 200 miles, during which they were to follow the radio range signal to Sonora. Don's ETA over the Sonora radio cone of silence was two hours. Half way through the first leg, the weather deteriorated. Lt. Stine had cautioned his students several times to be on the lookout for quick-forming Texas thunderstorms. Cadets were instructed to avoid flying into the storms, and were told to immediately turn back to base if they encountered such weather.

This night the clouds thickened and in no time lightning began to flash around the plane. Pete urged Don to reverse his course, but Don's confidence over-rode his judgment and he pressed on. The radio range signal they had been following faded out. Don checked his compass and held to a 90-degree heading, and assured his frustrated co-pilot that they were right on course. Two hours into the flight, Don looked hard for the lights of Sonora, but none were visible!

"Damn! We should have been right over the town by now. Pete, see if you can spot anything."

"Are you serious?" Pete shot back. "I haven't seen the damn ground in over an hour! We're obviously off course. When that range signal cut out, I knew we were in deep shit."

"Okay, I'm going to take her down and see if we can pick up some lights," Don shouted over the noisy engines.

They descended to three thousand feet. "Look," Pete yelled. "There she is, over to the right."

"That has to be Sonora," Don shot back.

"Man, I hope so," bellowed Pete.

The storm clouds forced them lower as the rain beat relentlessly against their windshield. Circling the lights, they looked for any landmark that would define their location. Since it was Friday night, Don figured there would be a high school football game in progress. He hoped to spot stadium lights or perhaps a high standing water tower.

Pete spotted a red light. Don lowered to five hundred feet, did a forty-five degree banking turn around the tower and saw large black letters, spelling out Sonora. Relieved to know their position, he turned to a hundred and eighty degree heading and climbed back up into the overcast sky. "That right engine doesn't sound right," Pete growled.

"Right. Lets keep an eye on the manifold and oil pressure gauges," Don retorted. Del Rio lay one hundred miles due south. Storm clouds continued to roll toward them from the east. They calculated it would take another fifty minutes to reach Del Rio. Ten minutes passed, and the right engine began to sputter. Pete looked out his window and saw the propellers slowing down. "We've got trouble out there with that one!"

"You're telling me," Don shouted back. "Look at those damn pressure gauges, they're all in the red! Let's feather that engine."

"Oh shit," Pete retorted. "We'll never make it to Del Rio if we shut her down!"

"We have to—otherwise we'll vibrate the engine right off the wing!"

Working quickly, Pete feathered the prop and turned off the switch. The propeller stopped wind milling and Don set the trim tabs to maintain altitude. Pete was showing his nervousness but his confidence was bolstered by Don's quick reactions and resolute spirit.

"Pete, see if you can raise Del Rio radio. If you can't get 'em, try our guarded emergency frequency."

Pete turned the dial to the Del Rio frequency and issued his call letters. No answer. He tried again, but still nothing. Frantically, Pete switched to the emergency frequency. "Mayday, Mayday!" he shouted. "This is Air Force four-five-zero, do you read? Over." The radio crackled with static. Pete repeated his call. This time he received an answer. "Aircraft in distress, what is your position?"

"This is Air Force four-five-zero. We're approximately fifty miles north of Del Rio. One engine is out, and we're unable to contact Del Rio radio for an emergency landing clearance."

"Roger, Air Force four-five-zero. This is Kerrville Air Force station. Turn to nine-zero degrees from your present heading, and you'll be on course for Rock Springs. It's ten miles from your present position. There's an emergency field on the edge of town. We'll notify them to turn on the field landing lights. Acknowledge."

Don grabbed the mike and replied, "Roger, Kerrville, we copy. We'll contact you when we have the runway lights in sight."

Don struggled to maintain his heading in the forceful wind that held them in its wake—slowing his craft to a mere 90 miles per hour. Don was slowly losing altitude, and the plane pitched and yawed from side-to-side. Pete was straining to see the lights of the field. "There," Pete yelled, pointing to his right. "I can see the blue runway lights. We're about five miles out."

Don turned toward the lights, calmly took the mike in hand and said, "Kerrville, this is Air Force four-five-zero, over."

"Air Force four-five-zero, go ahead."

"Kerrville, I have the field in sight. We're five miles west and are descending for a straight-in approach," Don advised. No sooner had he completed the transmission when the left engine sputtered and coughed. Don looked at Pete and smiled that cocky smile. "If this engine doesn't hold we'll have our first dead-stick landing, old buddy. We're going to get real close to those lights and glide her in."

The real test was at hand; to survive, they both had to work in unison. Don pushed the left throttle full forward in hopes of getting enough airspeed to make it to the landing strip. He decided not to call Kerrville until the engine quit totally. "Say a prayer Pete, and keep your eyes on those lights."

Two minutes passed as they approached the field. The engine gave its last sputter and died.

"Feather that sucker, Pete," Don yelled as he put the ship into a slow glide toward the runway.

The altimeter needle was winding downward. Don had to decide whether to go in wheels up or to lower the gear. At the last minute, Don dropped the wheels, and as the gear locked into position, they were down to only two hundred feet. The eerie sound of the wind filled the cockpit as they streaked toward the blue lights. The landing lights illuminated the swirling raindrops, decreasing their visibility.

"Brace yourself," Don yelled, as he broke his glide. Pete dropped his head forward, resting it below the instrument panel. Don hauled back on the yoke to bring the tail down. The squelch of the wheels as they made contact with the asphalt runway was music to their ears. They finally came to rest near the end of the strip.

"God, we made it," Pete sighed.

"We can thank the good Lord for that," Don muttered. At the same time Don wondered if fate had played a role again in his young life.

Anxious to continue the flight back to their base, they quickly called Kerrville for assistance. Kerrville informed them that help would have to be authorized by Eagle Base and that further instructions would be forthcoming. Don acknowledged, and then sat back in disgust. Both men agreed that they were in a heap of trouble, and they feared their consequences—when and if they ever got back to Eagle Air Force Base.

Seven

A n hour after their forced landing, the beleaguered cadets watched a repair truck pull alongside their plane. Two middle-aged staff sergeants jumped out with tool kits in hand. One slid a ladder out of the truck, as Don stuck his head out of the pilot's side window to welcome the coverall-clad mechanics. After a brief exchange, the mechanics detached the cowling from the left engine and began a routine engine inspection. They removed the spark plugs, dried them and screwed them back into the cylinder heads. They drained some fuel from each wing tank, then signaled Don to start the left engine. The engine coughed and turned over slowly before roaring into a speedy rotation. After the engine had run at full power for a few minutes, the mechanics motioned Don to shut it down.

The mechanics repeated the process on the other side of the plane, and the right engine coughed itself back to life and also ran smoothly. Satisfied that the engines were now performing as they should, the senior staff sergeant addressed the young airmen. "Too much moisture formed in your fuel tanks, fellas; drowned out the plugs. We've topped those wing tanks, but run those engines up for a couple more minutes. If those manifold and oil pressure gauges stay in the green, you'll be safe to go."

"Much obliged for the quick service, men," Don yelled over the roar of the engines.

The storm clouds had moved out, and in minutes the two weary birdmen were homeward bound on what turned out to be a happily uneventful, final leg of their original flight plan. After a smooth landing at Eagle Air Base, they taxied up to the ramp where their unhappy instructor was awaiting their arrival. They parked quickly, set the brakes, signed the plane's log and scrambled out of the ship. They approached the frowning Lt. Stine with a smart salute. "Sorry we're a little late in getting back, Sir," Don said half-jokingly.

Unmoved, Stine raised an eyebrow and spoke sternly. "Why didn't you turn back when you ran into that thunderhead, Mister?"

"Sir, I thought I could get around it. Then when we found Sonora, I figured we'd easily pick up Del Rio when I turned south," Don replied.

"You had to know the storm was coming from the east and it was bound to plague you all the way south, didn't you?" Stine pressed.

"Since our weather is generally always from the southwest, it seemed that the storm would eventually move to the northeast and we'd be out of it. Guess I miscalculated Sir."

"Yes, you did!" Stine shot back.

In his defense, Don took another approach. "Sir, I'm not sorry I did what I did. If I hadn't gone on, I would never have learned some valuable lessons."

"And just what were they?" Stine demanded.

"Well, if I had been on a real combat mission, I wouldn't have turned back. And I had an opportunity to experience a dead-stick landing at night."

Stine's angry, squinting eyes drilled into Don as he snapped back, "Look Mister Jennings, with the help of ground support you luckily got it down. Do you realize what a chance you took? You could have augured that plane in and killed both of you! That would have been a loss of a good aircraft as well. And you caused a lot of people trouble getting you back here. You've made me and our entire training program look bad. It looks like we're giving kids not smart enough to come in out of the rain expensive airplanes to play with—like we're not even teaching you the basics. I guess I'm guilty of assuming that when they send us a warm body it has a brain."

Stine paused, leaned back and his face relaxed, albeit with a clear frown of disgust remaining. Then he continued, voice rising with each word. "For failing to follow my pre-flight instructions, you both are confined to the base for the week-end. You will report Saturday at 0600 hours to the flight line to walk a four-hour tour--- with your parachutes strapped to your asses!" "Dismissed!"

Stine's dressing down made Don feel more than sad; Don was sick. The disciplinary action was the first either Don or Pete had received since entering the flight program. With his head slightly bowed, apologetically, Don turned to Pete. "I feel like a piece of shit. I'm sorry I got you into this mess buddy. Stine knows it was me, not you. At least he's not putting anything on our record. We just lose the weekend, eat shit and its over." Pete just shook his head. But Pete's reaction did not make Don feel any better; instead his feelings of guilt grew all the heavier. He wondered how he'd ever find favor with this instructor again. For the first time Don suspected he was getting too cocky for his own good.

When Monday morning arrived, and it was time to report back on duty, Don and Pete were feeling pretty embarrassed, and were worn out from their walking tour and the emotional wringing of their hands over the weekend. But time heals, and it seems the younger and cockier, the quicker it accomplishes its job. Within two weeks Don and Pete had managed to laugh off their punishment and life was as it was before Don challenged the thunderhead. Lt. Stine, to his credit and their relief, never mentioned the incident again.

In the final days of his training, Don teamed up with Pete Allen once again for a daylight, three hundred mile, low-level cross-country flight. While maintaining an altitude of fifty feet, the only "legalized buzzing" permitted during a cadet's training, they would dodge windmills, water towers, bridges and high rising landmarks scattered throughout the Rio Grand Valley. And though some felt uneasy because of the life-threatening hazards involved with flying low over unfamiliar terrain, most cadets looked forward to this final stage of their training, knowing it would culminate in their graduation. Don had a fighter pilot mentality and was anxious to fly the course. He hoped to polish his flying skills and prove he was worthy for assignment to twin-engine fighters upon graduation.

Almost before they knew it, the time had come and they were in the air. At great heights it's sometimes hard to estimate ground speed by eye; if you are high enough it seems as if you are hardly moving. At the other extreme, flying just above the ground was a bit like riding a roller coaster—only much faster. And with no open runway in front of you, things seemed to just shoot by. Residents of this part of the country were mostly cattle ranchers or citrus fruit growers, many of whom had often complained about the low-flying aircraft. The noise spooked the cattle and frightened migrant field workers. But as the two cadets flew this perilous flight, Don found himself grinning when he saw some workers dive for cover at the sight of his plane sweeping toward them in the wide-open field. He had the feeling of a war-like strafing mission, and these nervous field hands were the imaginary enemy soldiers. One minute he was cruising over fields and the next he was flying down the Rio Grand River, so low that more than one fisherman jumped from their boats into the water. The innocent victims had either miscalculated Don's true altitude or feared he was about to crash.

The low-level cross-country flight went without a hitch, giving Don and Pete even more confidence and pride as they neared graduation. But one more test was required. Once a cadet accumulated the required hours of flight time, he would be given the final check ride. When Don reached that checkout stage he was raring to go. He climbed into the cockpit with full confidence that he could handle any situation the examiner threw at him. As soon as Don took off and was barely two hundred feet above the ground, the check pilot pulled back both throttles and simply said, "forced landing." Don immediately dropped the nose, dumped ten degrees of flaps and glided straight forward. The instructor pushed both throttles forward, saying, "Just wanted to see if you'd try to kill us by attempting to turn back to the runway Mr. Jennings."

"Yes, Sir," Don replied as he continued his climb out of the traffic pattern.

"Can you show me a two-turn spin in this thing, Mister?"

"At what altitude, Sir?"

"Take her up to eight thousand."

Reaching the prescribed altitude, Don trimmed the plane for level flight and cautiously surveyed the area to assure himself there were no other planes below. Applying full power, he pulled back on the yoke and climbed steeply upward until the "Wichita Wobbler" shuddered convulsively and lost all forward lift. Kicking the left rudder to the floorboard, the plane dropped off clumsily and dove into a wildly, spinning turn.

Don yanked back the throttles. The falling craft made two full revolutions before Don kicked the right rudder and neutralized the controls. He strained, pulling back hard on the yoke to bring the nose up. Quickly applying full power to the quieted engines, he eased the diving craft slowly upward. Reaching eight thousand feet again, he leveled off and awaited his next command.

"All right, Jennings. Let's go home."

"Yes Sir," Don said happily.

Back on the ground, the check pilot took his time filling out the plane's Form One. Don was anxious to hear the final word about his check ride. He sat staring out the window for several minutes, which seemed to Don like at least an hour. Then, gently slapping Don on the knee, the instructor turned toward him and smiled. "That was a good ride Mister Jennings. Looks like you're ready for the bigger stuff. Now let's get out of this airplane and get a Coke."

For the first time Don felt like an equal to his instructors. He had proven his ability to fly an airplane as well as they did. As he walked back from the Post Exchange, where he had downed a Coke for the first time with a ranking officer, Don ran into Lt. Stine. "How'd you do on your check ride, Jennings?"

"I creamed it, Sir," Don boasted.

"I knew you would. And you might like to know, I've recommended you for twin-engine fighter school, since that was your request. But one last piece of advice Mister Jennings; whatever you do, don't let that cockiness get out of hand. It could kill you."

Don shook Stine's hand and thanked him for seeing him through his advanced training days. Then he was off to telephone Betty of his great news.

A week before Graduation Day, the instructors sponsored a moonlight party. And a memorable party it was. For Don, and likely for most of the cadets, everything and everyone seemed to have changed—as all personnel, instructors and the almost-former cadets alike, saw each other in a new light. The night air echoed with the strains of the familiar Air Corps song the young men knew so well. They had sung that song throughout their rigid training days, while going to class or marching to the parade grounds for inspection, but they would remember hearing it tonight.

Off we go...into the wild blue yonder,
Climbing high...into the sun.
Here they come...zooming to meet our
thunder,
At 'em boys...give'er the gun!
Down we dive...spouting our flame
from under,
Off with one...helluva roar!
We live...in fame
Go down...in flame, Hell!
Nothing can stop the Army Air Corps!

Spirits were upbeat, but there were melancholy moments too. All knew they would soon go their separate ways, and they would be going into the combat arena. Most would never see each other again. At one point, a trio of cadets broke out singing the "Whiffenpoof Song."

We're poor little lambs, who have gone
astray,
Baa baa baa.
Gentlemen songsters off on a spree
doomed from here to eternity,
May God have mercy on such as we,
Baa baa baa.

The frolicking went on until two o'clock in the morning. The cadets drew straws to see who would have clean-up duty, and as luck would have it, Don and Pete won the job. This night Don didn't seem to mind at all.

The following week was filled with preparations for the graduation exercises. The ceremony was rehearsed on the parade grounds, and cadets were shown where their families and friends would be seated. Then graduation day finally arrived.

The flag-draped speaker's stand was jammed with dignitaries. A band played as the crowd of families, friends and sweethearts looked on. With his recently acquired knowledge, experience and training under his belt, Don looked with new eyes at the aerobatics of the Air Review flown by underclassmen. To Don this was a proud miracle of formation flying. And finally, after too many speakers offered appropriate and relevant thoughts that went mostly unheard, they came to the ceremony's finale. One by one, the cadets stepped up to be presented their wings by Squadron Commanders. Civilians and underclassmen alike roared out the Air Force song with pride and patriotism—capturing all their pent-up feelings of what this moment meant to them. And when Betty pinned on his silver pilot wings, this day became the proudest one in Don's young life.

Eight

*F*ollowing the graduation ceremony, shipping notices were posted for the graduates. Don was ordered to twin-engine transitional fighter training at Fresno, California. Betty returned to Hemet in anticipation of their wedding date.

Upon reporting to Fresno, Don was placed in a training squadron under the command of Colonel Joe Bates, a decorated night fighter pilot of the war in Europe. Within days, Don was at the controls of a P-61 night fighter. The unique plane was nearly fifty feet long, fourteen feet high and had a wingspan of sixty-six feet. The plane was radar-equipped and flew at speeds exceeding four hundred miles per hour.

Don completed his checkout in the fighter, and was assigned a radar operator, Lieutenant Jerry Hurwitz. Jerry was jovial, witty and intelligent, and Don believed they would make a good team. Protocol meant that the new crewmen would share a room at the bachelor officer quarters. Don and Jerry quickly became close friends.

Flying became more rigorous, with long night target missions lasting until dawn. Squadron flight crews competed in locating and scoring the highest number of hits on elusive target planes. When they were down to their last scheduled night mission and feeling stressed, tired and weary from their rugged schedule, they decided to head to the officer's club. They would have a drink, to take the edge off, before this last flight. Inside the club they ran into Colonel Bates, who immediately asked if they were flying a mission that night.

"Yes Sir," Don spoke up, knowing that the Colonel already knew they were.

"Well then, I advise you to abstain from alcohol before you fly."

Both men felt a little miffed. As soon as Bates left, they looked at each other and grinned.

"Can you believe that?" Don said. "He thinks we're a couple of kids that can't handle our beer!"

"Yeah, sounds like it."

"Look," Don began, "one beer won't hurt us. Besides, he'll never know."

"Well, if you think we can get away with it, I'm game," Jerry responded.

They sipped their beers with their backs to the doorway, so they did not see Colonel Bates re-enter the bar. Stepping up beside Don, Bates barked, "Gentlemen, I thought I just told you both not to drink that stuff before your flight."

Though embarrassed, Don mustarded up a healthy dose of his abundant confidence and looked Bates in the eye.

"Yes, Sir, you did but I really didn't think one beer would harm us, since take-off is two hours away. We'll piss that out of our system long before then."

Jerry saw Bates's face redden.

"Lt. Jennings, you have potential to be a good fighter pilot. But you've apparently forgotten that you're a soldier. Soldiers do not disobey commands. My final warning to both of you is that you do not drink twenty-four hours before a flight. Is that clear?"

"Yes Sir, and I'm sorry for not realizing that you had given a command, Sir, rather than just advice. It won't happen again, Sir," Don quickly added, as he pushed his half-empty beer glass toward the bartender.

"Sir, that goes for me too," Jerry chimed in.

"All right then, let's order a coke and we'll forget the whole matter," Bates concluded. Raising his glass, Bates offered a toast.

"To tonight's interdictions, may the best crew win!"

"Here, here," Don and Jerry shouted in unison. Downing their cokes, the three walked out of the club side-by-side. When Colonel Bates disappeared around the next building, both men burst out laughing. But underlying their thoughts was the fact that they had disrespected Colonel Bates. Both were thinking that as officers they needed to be totally responsible and to act like leaders.

This mission was both dangerous and of huge importance in their training evaluations; it was their chance to take the squadron's top honors. They would fly over the Pacific Ocean in a simulated scouting mission to search for enemy aircraft. Target planes were flown both from land and from a carrier stationed eight hundred miles off the coast. The training squadron crews were to fire "dummy" bullets at as many target aircraft as they could. The targets were dubbed "pinball" planes and were equipped with electronic devices that registered every soft-nosed plastic bullet that struck them. This final gunnery score, combined with the previous mission scores, would determine the top crew.

Don and Jerry took off just after sunset. They headed west to seek out their evasive prey. Jerry was glued to his radarscope. His job was to spot the target aircraft and direct Don to the proper heading for interception. But for the longest time nothing seemed to be out there. After four hours, Jerry was beginning to think they were off course. Don insisted otherwise. Finally blips appeared on the scope.

"Bogies at nine o'clock. Steer two-niner-zero," Jerry shouted over the intercom.

"How far out, Jerry?"

"Estimate five minutes."

"Okay buddy. I'm locked on 'em; I'll give a burst when you give me the go ahead."

"You're zeroing in on them, but turn two degrees right and your lead will be enough to do it," Jerry advised. Don eased the craft slightly to the right. Jerry shouted again.

"Now, give them a burst."

They watched the streaking laser-like stream hit the target.

"Scratch one bogie," Jerry yelled. "We were right on the money."

The danger level was high in the flat ebony of night. As the black birds flew without outboard lights, they were invisible in the night skies, and mid-air collisions could occur, especially if radar blips gave a marred image. And now the danger increased as numerous "pinballs" as well as P-61's showed up in the area.

"Bogie at three o'clock," Jerry yelled again. Don banked sharply to pick up a ninety-degree heading.

"This baby is heading right for us. Are you gonna go for a head-on shot?" Jerry shouted.

"No better time than now," Don answered.

"Okay then, no course correction is needed. Just wait till I tell you to fire." A minute passed and Jerry gave the order. Don burst the bullets and instantly realized he was nearing a head-on collision. He pushed the yoke full forward.

Moments later the target plane zoomed over them, its belly just a few feet above them.

"Jerry," he yelled. "Did we get him?"

"Jesus Christ, Don, you almost crashed into him! Yeah you got him and I'll bet you scared the shit out of him too!"

"He closed in on us so fast there was nothing else I could do. Why didn't you warn me that he was so damn close?"

"My scope was getting two different blips. The other craft must have crossed over the target plane. My DMD was unable to handle them both at once," Jerry informed Don.

"Well, that one was too close for comfort. Let's hope we don't run into that situation again," Don said as he wiped sweat from his brow.

Two direct hits in one night made Don feel they were scoring well, but he still wanted to continue even though his fuel gauges were indicating half-empty. "Just one more would put the frosting on the cake," he told himself. "Get me another target Jerry," he urged. Jerry remained silent.

"Hey, did you hear me, buddy?" Don asked.

"Yeah I heard you but something screwy is going on. The scope is showing double blips everywhere. I know we don't have that many planes up here. These must be false signals."

"So you can't distinguish which ones are friendly and which aren't?" Don wanted to know.

"That's the gist of it. Our IFF must be out. No use firing on our own ships."

"You're right, Jerry. In real life we could not fire without identifying friend or foe. But tonight we don't have real bullets; and we're being graded on the number of hits on target ships. If we hit one of our guys nothing happens, so it seems to me that we could get another score or two if we just go after and shoot at whatever is out there. Hmmm. But on second thought, this exercise is to simulate the real thing, and shooting at all the planes would just be wrong. Yep. Let's head for home and call it a night."

"Yeah let's. Maybe we'll get lucky on the way back," Jerry joked.

Don reversed their course. Then Jerry shouted out once more.

"Bogie showing at two o'clock. Its about three miles from us."

"What the hell? Why is the IFF working now, when it didn't work back there when we saw all those blips? Well, whatever. Let's go for it," Don eagerly replied.

As they drew closer to the target, Don had a strange feeling.

Over the last hour the stratospheric clouds had thinned and moved out, turning the night from black to a hazy gray. The silhouette of a plane etched into view and Don's sharp eye quickly identified it as a P-61. As he moved in for a closer look he noticed only one engine exhaust flame.

"Jerry, switch to the emergency frequency. I have this bogie in sight now and he appears to be in trouble."

Instantly they heard a distress call; "May Day! May Day! This is Air Force eight-zero-zero. Over."

"Air Force eight-zero-zero, this is five-six-zero, what is your altitude and position?" Don asked calmly.

"Five-six-zero, I'm at twelve thousand on a heading of ninety degrees, two hundred miles west of Santa Barbara. Over."

"Air Force eight-zero-zero, we have you in sight. We're five hundred yards behind you. Over."

"We've lost one engine and my number two is loosing manifold pressure. Request you stand by in case we have to ditch out here. Over."

"Are you heading for Fresno, eight-zero-zero?" Don asked.

"That is correct. This is Squadron Commander Bates. Who might you be?"

"Lieutenant Don Jennings, Commander Bates. We'll follow you back to base."

"How far to the coast, Jerry?" Don asked.

"Picking up the shoreline now. I'd say we should be there in thirty minutes. At this speed we'll make it to base in forty-five minutes."

As Don throttled back to keep alongside his lumbering charge, his earphones filled with the urgency-intoned voice of Colonel Bates; "Jennings, we've just lost our instrument panel lights. Do you read me? Over."

"I read you Colonel. I'll pull out in front of you. Follow my engine exhausts. If your radio fails, stay on our tail and we'll guide you right down to

76

the runway. Let me know when you've got us in full view. Over."

Bates caught sight of Don's blue-flamed exhausts and quickly responded. "I've got you, Jennings. I can't see my altimeter; I'll follow you in. Over."

"Roger, Colonel. How does it look?"

"If this engine holds up, we'll make it."

"We'll be over the field in about fifteen minutes Colonel."

Bates acknowledged then switched to his intercom to talk to his crewmate, Lieutenant Mike Ross. "Better get your flotation vest on Ross, we may have to ditch."

"I'm way ahead of you sir. I put my vest on as soon as you feathered that number one engine," Mike replied.

When they were safely past the coastline, Don breathed a sigh of relief, and then he called for a straight in approach landing at Fresno. He urged Jerry to keep an eye on Bates as they lowered for the landing. Now at five hundred feet, Bates strained to keep his airplane from getting too close to his guide. Suddenly his right engine quit!

"He's coming in dead stick!" Jerry yelled.

"Is his gear down?" Don asked.

"Not that I can see."

Seconds later Don landed and rolled down the runway.

Bates eased back on the yoke in an effort to stretch his glide. At the edge of the runway his plane stalled out and slammed hard into the asphalt runway. The plane skidded several hundred yards. Sparks flew in all directions. Halfway down the strip the huge fighter finally screeched to a halt, and in seconds burst into flames.

From his vantage point Jerry observed one figure jump from the wreckage and race for safety. The flames engulfed the ship instantly. "She caught fire, Don. One guy got out of her!" Jerry exclaimed.

As Don taxied back toward the wreckage, the fire crews were spraying the plane with foam. The flames reached the wing tanks and a violent explosion erupted tossing two of the fire fighters into the air. The firemen backed away from the blazing inferno and stood watching.

Don and Jerry rushed to the scene to see Commander Bates among the corps of firemen. "Are you okay Commander?" Don asked.

"I'm all right Lieutenant...but Lieutenant Ross didn't make it out. I'll see you in the morning Lieutenant." Bates turned and walked slowly from the scene.

Jerry stood gazing at the burning wreckage, shocked at the thought of losing a fellow radar operator. The two had attended radar school together and had gone through transitional training in the P-61 squadron. Mike was the first friend Jerry had lost since he had enlisted, and the reality of the hazards he faced in his line of work became all too clear.

Nine

The following day, Don reported to Commander Bates. "Good morning Sir. You wanted to see me?"

"Yes, Lieutenant Jennings. You did a fine job in leading me in last night...without your help I couldn't have stayed with that ship. I thought we could bring it in safely. Perhaps it was the wrong decision, but bailing out over the Pacific at night didn't seem to be the better option. These are the choices we have to make in this business, and we sometimes make the wrong ones. Now we need to concentrate on the business at hand. There will be a memorial service for Lieutenant Ross at the base chapel tomorrow at 9 a.m."

"Lieutenant Hurwitz and I will be there Sir," Don replied.

"On another item, Lieutenant, I've just read the reports from our mission last night. Your ship scored the most target hits, which makes you top gun in the squadron. Congratulations."

"Thank you Sir. I couldn't have done it without my OR, Jerry Hurwitz."

"Both of you will receive a letter of commendation, Lieutenant. And one more thing...our squadron has been designated as combat-ready and we will soon receive shipping orders for the Pacific Theater. If you have any last minute affairs to clean up, I suggest you do them soon."

"As a matter of fact, Colonel Bates, there are a few things I have to do. Most importantly is my wedding! I'm going to ask Chaplin Crosby to conduct the ceremony at the base chapel. Would you attend, Sir?"

"Be happy to Jennings. Just let me know the date. Now I must get back to work. You're dismissed."

Don saluted and left. On his way back to his quarters he couldn't help wondering why Colonel Bates was so cold-hearted about Ross's death. Don asked himself; "Does he look upon Ross as just another number? Is that what I am to Bates too— just a number? Or is it that squadron commanders must keep their true feelings from their official duties?" Don didn't know the answers, but he decided to reserve judgment on Bates.

Don lost little time in calling Betty to give her the news of his likely short shipping date to the Pacific and to discuss immediate wedding plans. Betty agreed to have the wedding at the base chapel. The next morning Don contacted the Chaplin who readily agreed to perform the wedding ceremony on the following weekend.

During the next day's memorial services for Mike Ross, Don sensed Jerry's bereavement. After the service Don suggested they stop off at the officer's club, where he hoped he could lighten Jerry's mood. Don began with the news of their becoming top guns in their squadron, something that should make any airman jump off of his seat. Jerry seemed unimpressed. Don pursued his effort to engage Jerry. "Yah know buddy," Don began, "for as long as we've known each other, we have never shared our thoughts on our religious beliefs. You're Jewish and I was raised in the Christian faith. Don't both of our religions teach that there's a life after this one?…So Mike's in a better place right now."

"I guess so…but I don't really know," Jerry said rather sadly.

"I went to Sunday School and Church when I was growing up and it was all about Christ's life, death and resurrection. Does your religion teach there's a heaven?"

"I'm not the best guy to ask about the Jewish religion. I haven't practiced it much since my bar mitzvah, when I was twelve years old. But I do believe in the God of Moses."

"Our Bible tells us that story too, Jerry. We were both taught there is one God and He loves us. If He loves us then He'll take care of us."

"I was told our Torah is about the same as your Old Testament Bible. So He's up there looking down on us and looking out for us...but why'd He take Mike and not me?" Jerry asked.

"Mike was in the wrong seat, is my guess. Some of God's creatures live a longer life than others. It's a mystery for sure. Faith in a God does make it easier to get through tragedies, like we've seen already, Jerry."

"Thanks for trying to make me feel better. I know I have to get over Mike's death. And I can't keep thinking it could happen to me, like it did to Mike, or I'll be worthless as your OR."

"One thing for sure, God didn't make these airplanes. If we want to fly 'em it's the chance we take. Trust me, you will get over this, just like I had to when I lost my roommate and instructor."

Jerry nodded, swilled down his beer, and ordered a second one.

"Well, friend," Don perked, "how about helping me out in this wedding. Wanta be my best man?"

"Man, I thought you'd never ask," Jerry said half-heartedly.

"Atta boy, partner. I knew you wouldn't let me down. Listen, I've already talked to the Chaplin, and the dates for next Saturday. All you need to do is round up some of the guys. Betty will invite her parents and some of her friends and hopefully, my folks will be here. We'd better get off our duffs and snap to buddy; we're down to the wire on this one!"

The days flew by, and Betty arrived at the train station on schedule. She hurriedly stepped down onto the loading platform as Don bounded towards her with open arms. Jerry was amused at the sight of Don racing to his bride-to-be. He wondered if he would ever feel this way about a woman. He couldn't imagine it.

Don lifted Betty off her feet and carried her a few steps before putting her down. All that they had been anticipating for so long was about to become a reality. After a long embrace and a kiss, Betty turned toward Jerry.

"You must be Jerry. I've heard so much about you."

"Hi sweetheart," Jerry replied with a big smile.

"Are we all set for Saturday, Don?" Betty asked.

"Jerry thinks we are, and he believes we can pull this off without a rehearsal. What do you think Honey?" Don jostled.

"Oh, I know we can, Betty added confidently. But let's not think about it anymore, or we'll start getting nervous and foul things up."

Grabbing Betty's luggage, Don lead the way and set off for the hotel where he had reserved rooms for Betty and for his parents.

Jennings' parents arrived on Friday. It had been two years since they had seen their son, and emotions flowed uncontained. It was also the time to meet the prospective bride, which folded in warmly among the tears of joy. Betty's parents joined the happy couple.

As Jerry observed the reunion, he choked up at the sight of the families greeting each other. He hadn't seen his parents in the last two years either; they couldn't leave their store due to the shortage of help, as the war effort had gobbled up the labor market for industrial support. And now Jerry didn't expect to see them until his overseas assignment was completed, which would be another couple of years—if he survived.

The wedding came off as planned. Betty was radiant in her long white gown, and Don and Jerry were as handsome as movie stars in their formal officer dress. Upon completion of their vows, the nuptials exited the chapel to pass through a military tribute of crossed-swords, extended by fellow officers. The small reception was a class act, and a credit to Jerry's management expertise. The modest dinner was delicious, and the twenty guests managed to consume over thirty bottles of wine and champagne.

Following the ceremony Don was given a five-day furlough. The couple motored off with Don's parents to a breath-taking view of Yosemite National Park. Especially appropriate for the newly weds was the sight of Bridal Veil Falls. And when the festive time ended, the couple saw Jim and Maggie Jennings off, as they set out for home in a bittersweet goodbye.

The newly weds spent two more days together, their only two alone as husband and wife, before shipping orders came for the squadron to immediately deploy overseas. Don's last precious memory of Betty was her waving a tearful goodbye, as he boarded a transport ship and headed out of the harbor in San Francisco Bay.

Ten

While Don lay in a body cast, facing an unknown future and reminiscing over his past, Lieutenant Jordan Bond was also reminiscing. As Jordan sat patiently watching the rescue team working high up on the mountain, he reflected on the series of events and decisions that had brought him to this moment in time. He remembered when he had first heard about the cadet pilot training class being formed at Tuskegee Institute in 1941, exactly sixty years after the school had been founded by one of his childhood heroes, Booker T. Washington. Jordan was already an engineering student at Tuskegee, the best school in the world in Jordan's mind; but how prestigious would it be to be a fighter pilot in this future world of flight.

Jordan had enthusiastically applied for the flight training, and when he received his letter of acceptance he felt as if he were already flying, or at least walking on air. Jordan thought about how hard he had studied to earn his engineering degree in Tuskegee's Division of Aeronautics, and then how exciting it had been to be part of the AAF training there. Like the other cadets, once he had completed primary training at Tuskegee's Moton Field, he was sent to nearby Tuskegee Army Air Field for completion of flight training and for transition to combat-type aircraft. As part of the first classes of Tuskegee airmen, Jordan had been trained to be a fighter pilot for what would become the famous 99th Fighter Squadron, slated for combat duty in North Africa.

Like the other candidates who applied for the program, Jordan had also viewed the opportunity to become a flying officer as a means to attain social equality in the United States Army Air Corps. He had believed the prejudice and segregation would end, once he and his fellow cadets were commissioned. But instead, the graduates were formed into an all-Negro P-51 fighter squadron and lived in separate quarters from white crews.

As a member of the Red-tailed Squadron, Jordan flew cover for the 15th Air Force Bomber Group conducting raids as far north as Rumania. Along with escorting bomber flights daily, they scrambled to intercept approaching enemy aircraft.

Life in this squadron, at this time with this assignment, was both exciting and extremely life threatening. On his first scramble mission, Jordan intercepted a Messerschmitt 109 fighter escorting a German Dornier bomber. Fortunately for Jordan the light and his approach angle were just right, and he flew directly in for a shot. He watched his tracer bullets as they found their way into the rear of the cockpit. The 109 did a slow roll and spiraled downward in flames. Losing little time, Jordan turned toward the DO 17 Dornier. He quickly overtook the twin-engine bomber and blasted away at the fleeing bomber's wing tanks. The plane exploded in mid-air and fell into the sea.

Elated initially, Jordan soon felt remorseful. He had just killed several men who were his worthy adversaries and counterparts. Furthermore, they were white men. A year ago, if he approached a white man in Alabama, he would have stepped down off the sidewalk to let the man pass. These brief feelings passed quickly as he told himself they were not germane or rational, and he became determined to add more victories to his credit. And only one week later he scored three more enemy kills, establishing him as a fighter ace. While his own squadron applauded his victories, the white flyers continued to ignore him.

But Jordan had developed a new world of his own in the sky; a world in which he was a master, and the enemy planes better look out. One day he slipped out of his flight formation and chased an enemy plane far into the French Alps. The retreating enemy turned out to be a decoy and Jordan was hit by five enemy fighters waiting high above him. Forced to bail out of his burning ship, Jordan maneuvered his chute and narrowly avoided the snow-capped peaks. He landed in a tree below the timberline.

He freed himself and dropped to the ground safely; retrieved his map of the Italian coast from his survival kit, and pinpointed his location. He quickly figured he'd have to get down this mountain and scale another one before he could descend to the sea, if he was ever to have a chance of returning to his base.

Nightfall was approaching, so he quickly gathered some firewood and found a nook in which to bed down. His trusty Zippo cigarette lighter came in handy and in minutes he had a blazing fire. The only food he had was two chocolate bars he had stuck into his flight jacket. As night fell, he stretched out by the fire and fell fast asleep.

When dawn came, Jordan awoke and headed up the slopes in a southerly direction. As he cautiously hiked up an ascending trail he heard voices in the distance. He quickly hid behind a tree. As the strangers approached, he detected a French accent. "Thank God they aren't Italians or Germans!" he thought to himself.

Two men and two women were in the party. Taking a chance, Jordan stepped out and met them face-to-face. The group came to an abrupt stop. One man carrying a gun pointed it at him. He quickly raised his hands and gestured that he meant them no harm. The man with the gun drew nearer. After looking Jordan over from head to toe, he broke into a smile.

"Do you speak English?" Jordan asked.

"Oui. What are you doing here Monsieur?" the Frenchman asked in an alarmed tone.

"I was shot down by the Germans yesterday. I'm trying to get back to my base in North Africa."

Turning to the others, the man spoke to them in French. An excited exchange commenced between them.

"Monsieur, do you have identification?"

Fumbling through his shirt, Jordan produced his dog tags from around his neck. Satisfied, the man smiled broadly and extended his hand. Jordan shook it enthusiastically.

"Monsieur, my name is Jacques Armand. This is my brother Joseph, and our wives, Rose Marie and Fifi. We are with the French resistance forces. We have just come back from escorting another flyer to safety. He was with a bombardment group near Benghazi. We can help you too. But first we must know where you want to go in North Africa."

"I know of that bomb group. My base is not far from there near Tripoli. Can you get me passage there once we climb over this mountain?" Jordan responded.

"Monsieur, it is a long climb. We have made this trip twice this month. If you are up to going, we have connections to get you passage across to

Tripoli. But it will not be easy. The Germans and Italians carefully watch the ports."

"I shall forever be indebted to you if I can get back to my base."

The small group started with Jacques in the lead. The women bantered back and forth in French. Joseph and Jacques were curious as to the type of aircraft Jordan had been flying. To Jordan's surprise, they seemed quite familiar with the American planes.

"It's no wonder you Americans can out-fly the Nazis!" Joseph said with a smile.

Night was approaching and the air was getting much colder as they neared the snow-covered peak. Jacques called a halt; he began giving orders. Soon the others were scurrying about in an orderly fashion. The women gathered dry wood while Joseph found an outcropping that would provide shelter for a campsite. A fire was started and Jacques produced a container of food—mostly dried, smoked fish. The portions were small but satisfying. After they had eaten, everyone bedded down. Rose Marie snuggled up beside Joseph, while Fifi nestled next to Jacques. Jordan had no blanket so he curled up near the fire and quickly fell asleep.

He was awakened by the sound of birds chattering just as the sun was rising. Soon the others awoke, passed around some dry, stale bread and strong, black coffee. Then they continued their climb. When they reached the summit, Jordan could see the Mediterranean Sea. As he moved along, he heard the women giggling behind him. Both of the women were attractive and looked enough alike to be sisters. When they stopped to rest, he found he couldn't keep his eyes off of Fifi, and she returned his stares. Jacques was busy looking at a map and appeared to be puzzled but said nothing. As they moved on, Jordan spoke to him.

"Are we going in the right direction?"

With a look of disdain, Jacques answered. "Are you questioning my sense of direction Lt. Bond?"

Jordan was troubled by this unfriendly response. "It's just that I saw you studying your map with a look of doubt back there a minute ago. I wondered if you had a problem," Jordan said reticently.

"I was merely checking for the best village to bring you into when we reach the coast. We never use the same village to rendezvous with our coastal contacts," he snapped.

Jordan felt uncomfortable with this exchange. Is it possible that he had caught him looking at his wife? Or, was he irked because he was tired? Whatever the reason, Jordan felt uneasy.

They would soon be down the mountain and Jordan knew the coastal villages could be occupied by Italian soldiers or even Germans. Nearing a village, Jacques halted the procession. He told Jordan to stay with the women while he and Joseph went ahead to make connections with the underground operatives.

As the men disappeared in the distance, Fifi spoke in English. "Lt. Bond, I am afraid for you!"

Stunned, Jordan stammered, "Why haven't you spoken in English before now? And why are you afraid for me?"

"Our husbands are not good Frenchmen," she answered. "They are collaborators for the enemy. They are going now to find the Italian military so they can turn you over to them. You must get away before they return!"

"But where will I go? I don't even know where I am. Surely you can tell me what direction to go!" Fifi stood up and threw her arms around him and held him for a moment.

"Oh Lieutenant, I don't want you to be taken captive. We will guide you to safety. We have to get away from these evil men too. We can no longer be a part of their treachery. We hate them!" Tears were running down her face. "We are sisters, Lt. Bond. These men have forced us to take part in their horrible deeds. Let us help you. We have friends in the village. But we have to go quickly," Rose Marie pleaded.

Jordan needed no further coaxing. Fifi led them into a barn near the edge of the village. It was dark inside, and the smell of horses filled their nostrils—the dusty odor reminded Jordan of his boyhood on the farm in Alabama.

"Please wait here until we return," said Fifi.

Jordan flopped down in the hay and dozed off. He was awakened by a hand on his shoulder. Fifi was alone. "Everything will be all right," she began. "Our friends are going to help us. They will hide us here till they can contact a ship captain who will take you to Tripoli."

"But what will happen to you and Rose Marie?" Looking sadly at him, Fifi spoke softly.

"We will hide here until we are sure Jacques and Joseph are gone. Then our friends will help us get back to our parents. We have been discussing this for some time, and now that they have taken us to this village with our friends, and now that you are in grave danger, we have decided to take the risk now and make our escape."

Gently, Fifi put her arms around Jordan. She looked down at him with the sadness of a little puppy. Jordan didn't want to let go of her. He drew her down beside him, kissing her tenderly. She melted in his arms as they locked in a loving embrace. "I don't know what has gotten into me. I want so much to make love to you!" Jordan blurted out. "Yes. Please," she uttered, and Jordan caressed her as they discarded their clothing.

Rose Marie had stayed at the farmhouse when Fifi went back to the barn. After nearly two hours passed, Rose Marie became anxious and made her way to the barn. Opening the door, she caught a glimpse of the two making love. She quickly closed the door and returned to the house. She felt a wave of jealousy. She too liked the handsome Lieutenant and wished that it could have been her nestled in his arms. She wondered if her sister would share him with her. She returned to the barn to find out.

As she entered the barn she coughed and bumped the door on purpose. Both of them sat up—

not bothering to cover themselves. Fifi called to her sister in French. Rose Marie sat down in the hay beside them. The two sisters began a quiet but earnest conversation. When it ended, Rose Marie stood up and stripped completely. She too, was endowed with a beautiful figure like that of her sister. Soon the two were sharing Jordan. And when the sexual frenzy ended, they all fell into a tranquil sleep.

When Jordan awoke, the women were gone. He had heard stories about how sensuous the French were, and he wondered if all the French women were like Fifi and Rose. He hoped this encounter would not distract them from their promise to get him to Tripoli.

Soon they both returned. They brought some food and red wine. He devoured it all like a starved animal, as Fifi spoke of her news. "Lieutenant, we will stay with you here tonight. By morning there should be a friend to take you to the captain of the boat. You must rest now so you are ready to make the journey."

"Tell me," Jordan asked. "Where are you from and how may I find you after we have kicked the hell out of the Italians and Germans?"

"We are from the village of Perot, just outside of Paris. Our parents live there now, and our family has always lived in that village for as long as anyone knows. Once we return home, we'll join up with the true French resistance forces. We'll fight till all the Nazis are gone from our homeland," Fifi vowed.

Rose Marie held his hand and added, "Lieutenant, we are so proud of you for fighting for our country. We shall never forget you. You must not worry about us. We have many good friends in the village. We will be taken care of until we can get back to our home. If you get to Paris someday, please come to see us. Our family name is Boy-ye."

Jordan took them both in his arms and they laid their heads on his shoulders and fell softly into sleep, which was soon to be interrupted. Someone was kicking his foot, and when Jordan awoke, he looked up into two rifles pointed at his head. Behind the rifles were the brash faces of Jacques and Joseph. In an instant, the women jumped to their feet.

"Don't move, any of you. So, you thought you could get away from us?" He smirked. "Get your clothes on, you stupid American!"

The women were frozen with fright. They looked at Jordan, who sensed their desperation. He knew the Frenchmen had just made a mistake by allowing him to dress. He quickly slipped on his pants and boots and waited for a chance to overpower them. It didn't take long.

Both husbands grabbed their wives; cursing and shaking them violently, and when they were reaching a peak of anger, Jordan kicked aside the hay and grabbed his pistol. He fired rapidly hitting his captors in the back. Both men crumpled into a heap on the barn floor. The women screamed in horror. He threw his arms around them and drew them tightly to him. "They would have killed all of us. They were like mad dogs when they discovered both of you with me. We must get out of here in case any of their compatriots come looking for them."

The women rushed Jordan into their friend's house and told them what had happened. Hurriedly the couple dashed to the barn to retrieve the bodies. They drug them to an abandoned well and dumped them in. When they returned, the couple and the girls led Jordan to a nearby harbor-house. When they entered the small house they were greeted by a friendly woman with silver hair. Fifi and Rose engaged her in conversation, then turned to Jordan.

"We must stay here until morning then you will be taken to the ship that departs for Tripoli. Rose Marie and I will be escorted back to our village very soon."

Early the next morning a man appeared to take him to the ship. Leaving his American uniform behind, Jordan donned a pair of black pants and a faded, striped red and white shirt that his new host provided. Jordan said his good-byes to Fifi and Rose.

The man led Jordan to a large cargo ship with strange markings. They boarded the vessel and Jordan was taken to quarters two decks below. His guide shook his hand and bid him good-bye.

After several hours he went up to the deck where he met a sailor who greeted him in English. "My name is Sebastian and this ship carries grain to Africa and flies the neutral flag. Of course we aren't supposed to transport soldiers, but we do. In fact, we have a German airman aboard now who is eager to rejoin his squadron. We will transport both of you to Tripoli and then you are on your own. How the Germans get their man out of Tripoli is up to them. Let's hope we don't get stopped and they find you guys," he confided.

"Tell me," Jordan asked, "Who will meet me in Tripoli to get me to my outfit?"

"I don't know. Someone always meets us to find out if we have someone they are interested in. We just get you to Tripoli, and that is our only concern."

Jordan was really hungry and inquired if he might have some food.

"Follow me. I'll take you to the galley."

The galley was tiny and dimly lit. As they entered, Sebastian said, "There's your enemy, over there."

Jordan saw a handsome, blond-headed young man in his early twenties. He decided he wanted to get to know him, so he asked Sebastian if they could sit with the German pilot.

Approaching the table, Sebastian spoke out, "Hello Heir Reichmann. Mind if we join you?"

"Not at all, Mr. Sebastian; please sit down."

"This is another fallen birdman," Sebastian said as they sat down.

"How do you do?" Reichmann said as he extended his hand.

"So we both are working our way back to our units. I never thought I'd be eating with the enemy on such friendly terms," Jordan began.

"Nor I. However, since we are in the same boat, so to speak, we can call a truce and enjoy the ride, can't we?"

"I agree wholeheartedly."

"You know, I've always wondered about the American "Tuskegee" boys. You've made quite a name for yourselves over here."

"I am proud to be a part of this squadron. We work very hard and we work well together."

"Well, I'll leave you two men to talk," Sebastian said as he graciously departed.

Jordan opened the discussion again. "How is it that you got here?"

"I was downed over the coast a few days ago. I had just shot down a P-51 over the Alps and was returning to my base. Three P-51's jumped me when I reached the coast. They got my left wing tank, and I had to jump. I was fortunate to hit the water, and I swam in."

Jordan was taken aback. "Could this be the son-of-a-bitch that got me?" he wondered.

"How did you happen to get the P-51?"

"Easiest one I've had. The guy was chasing one of our decoys. He didn't see us. We followed him about a thousand feet above and waited until he got far enough North so he was alone. Then I attacked him."

Jordan knew immediately that this was the pilot that shot him down. He looked at him for a moment and then he began to laugh, almost hysterically.

"Did you find my story amusing?"

"In a way, yes. You see Heir Reichmann, I'm the one you shot down! I never thought I'd meet the man who got me!"

"I understand now. I'm glad you survived. I hoped that you would, since I saw you go over the side of your plane."

"I'm not for killing the enemy either. I've never felt comfortable about it. On the other hand, I don't give a shit about the Nazi regime. I'm for kicking Hitler's bunch the hell out of Europe. As a pilot, I'm satisfied that we can win this war by knocking down as many of your aircraft as we can. I'm glad you survived too. Maybe sometime I'll get a chance to go up against you one-on-one, but at the same time I hope we do not have to kill each other."

"Yes, I can imagine that you would like to have a fair dog fight. Of course it will probably never happen. And we'd never know it if we did. But I know you'd give me a good fight."

Jordan did not hate him. Rather, he felt sorry for him. The Germans would never win this war. He felt that if this man ever returned to the air, it would only be a matter of time until he was shot down again.

When Sebastian returned, he told the pilots they had just a few hours until they docked. Jordan excused himself, went back to his quarters, and flopped into his hammock. Sleep came upon him instantly.

Hours later Sebastian knocked on his door and told him they would be docking in ten minutes. Up on deck, he met Reichmann again.

"It appears we will soon part company Heir Reichmann."

"I'm sure you'd rather we didn't Lieutenant. You probably would rather take me prisoner instead."

"As a matter of fact, I would. You could go home alive when the war is over."

Reichmann looked at him for a moment. It was plain that he felt a brotherly comradeship toward Jordan too. "Lieutenant, perhaps if we survive the war, we could be friends one day."

"I'd like nothing more. Meanwhile, take care of yourself and stay out of the way of those P-51's!"

The two men shook hands and Jordan made his way towards the port side of the ship. Sebastian appeared as the ship settled to a stop.

"Ah Bond, I'm glad you're here. This fellow will take you on shore. Good luck and stay healthy."

"Thank you Mr. Sebastian and God-speed. I won't forget you."

Jordan followed his appointed leader till they came to a small tavern at the edge of the city. The man motioned him inside, then poured them each a glass of red wine, downed his drink and left. Jordan assumed that he was to wait there.

His wait wasn't long. Two men came over to his table as soon as his escort had left. They appeared to be French also.

"Lieutenant, we know who you are and we are here to take you back to your base. Our car is outside. Don't ask any questions and we won't have to answer any. Just trust us to get you back. This duty is routine to us."

The bumpy ride took less than two hours. They pulled up to the sentry post beside the main gate. The car stopped and the men turned around and smiled.

"Lieutenant, you are home. May God take care of you." Jordan thanked them, bounded out of the car and headed for his headquarters. He hurried into the office. An orderly recognized him immediately.

"Lieutenant Bond!"

"None other. Is the Colonel in?"

"Yes Sir." He led him into the Commander's office. Colonel Davis Benjamin looked up. Jordan saluted and said, "Lieutenant Jordan Bond reporting for duty Sir!"

The Colonel returned the salute, stood up and looked him over from head to toe. "Lieutenant, you're a sight for sore eyes. We hoped you'd make it, but you have been listed as missing in action for some time. I'm glad you're back and I suppose you have a whopper of a story to tell!"

"Yes Colonel, but you'd never believe it!"

Eleven

ow, here on the mountain surrounded by white airmen, Jordan again found himself being ignored, as the medics dressed Jerry's scalp wound and bandaged Jill's ankle, and placed them on stretchers for evacuation. Until now, Jordan had never had a combat wound or been involved in a military accident. As the column moved out, Lieutenant Keaton motioned for Jordan to bring up the rear. Lou Fraley stayed close to Jill and Jerry as the party inched its way down the mountain, and Jordan resented being positioned at the end of the procession, the back of the bus so to speak, away from his two companion survivors.

Halfway down the mountain, the party came upon a clearing and Keaton ordered them to halt.

When they stopped, a shot rang out. Keaton fell to the ground, dead, with a bullet through his head. The others dove to the ground for cover as Lou Fraley flung himself over Jill's body.

Jordan dashed to the head of the column, pistol in hand. He focused on a tree only thirty or so yards away—a sniper, crouched in the fork of the tree, twenty feet up, was drawing a bead on another American soldier. Jordan quickly aimed and fired. The sniper tumbled out of the tree and landed head first on the ground.

Knowing he was the only able-bodied commissioned officer left, Jordan took command and shouted for everyone to stay down. Moments later Lou Fraley crawled up to Jordan's side.

"See anymore of them?" Fraley whispered.

"No movement at all. If they aren't behind those trees, then there's probably a patrol nearby."

"Christ! They've killed Lieutenant Keaton!" Lou exclaimed.

"I'm afraid so. He never knew what hit him."

Everyone stayed down for several more minutes. Bond concluded that the sniper was a scout and ordered the column to move out quickly. The rescuers wrapped Lt. Keaton's body in a blanket, placed him on a makeshift stretcher and moved on.

Ironically, Lt. Bond was leading the group now instead of bringing up the rear. No one objected. The nervous group seemed to move with much more agility and heightened readiness, expecting another, perhaps even more horrific, surprise attack. But without further encounter, the weary band reached the flat valley floor and it seemed no more time passed before they were inside the base complex.

Two hours after their arrival back at the base, Jill, aided by a cane, limped down the hallway. As she did, Jerry emerged from the x-ray room and informed her that he didn't have a skull fracture and would be fine in a couple of days. Jill confirmed that her injury was just a bad sprain. As they talked, Lt. Bond appeared and anxiously reported he had found Don.

"Where is he; what's his condition?" They both asked.

"He has a broken back."

The trio made their way down the hall and into the ward. The long room was empty except for Don, who was snoring lightly.

"Shall I wake him?" Jerry asked.

"Go ahead. I'm sure he won't mind when he sees who we are," Jordan urged.

Jerry shook Don's hand lightly. Don snored on. Jerry shook his hand a little harder, and Don groaned and opened his eyes.

"Jerry! You made it!" As he turned his head, he saw Jill and Jordan.

"Hey, are you both okay?"

"We're fine now, but what about you?" Jill asked in a shaky voice.

"I am a happy man because I'm looking at you guys. As far as my situation, well I guess this body cast tells it all. They say I broke my back. I fell down a waterfall. That's why it took so long for a rescue team to get back to you."

"You'll be back on your feet in no time," Jerry quipped encouragingly.

"I'm afraid that's not going to happen. The doctor's already told me I can't be treated here. They're going to transfer me to the States."

Jill's heart sank, and tears welled up in her eyes. She so longed to hold his hand and tell him how much she loved him. Instead she muttered something about having to go to the "little girl's room."

When she left, Don looked at Jerry and Jordan, gloomily. "Tell me, was it rough on her up there?"

Jerry answered. "It was a little rough. But the toughest part was the descent. Lt. Keaton was killed. We thought we were all goners, and would have been, if the enemy patrol had found us. Jill was a real trouper through it all."

"Keaton was killed?"

"Yes, by a sniper, but Jordan got the bastard," Jerry confirmed.

Don was stunned. He had known Lt. Keaton well. A wave of guilt came over him.

"Fellas, I apologize for the mess I got you in. I can't undo what has happened. I just want you to know how truly sorry I am. Please go and get some rest."

Sensing that Don wanted to be alone with Jill on her return, they nodded and left.

Jill limped to Don's bedside. Slowly she reached for his hand and held it tenderly.

"I've missed you, and I'm sorry to see you like this."

"I've missed you too, Jill. I tried to make it down that mountain as fast as I could; I guess too fast. I lost my footing. My life was spared by a native boy coming to my rescue."

"Don, I must ask you to level with me."

"Jill, I haven't stopped thinking about you since I left you up there!"

"Then why didn't you tell me you were married?"

Awkwardly Don tried to think of the words to explain. Looking into her tearful eyes, he tightened his hand around hers. "Jill, I know you aren't going to believe this, but I was going to tell you about my wife as soon as we were back from that flight. I've been wanting to tell you for days, brooding over it ever since I met you. You must believe me! I do love you Jill."

"I guess it really doesn't matter now anyway. We'll never be together again since they're sending you back to the States."

"Don't talk like that! It'll only be for a little while. You'll be coming home, or I'll be coming back out here. Nothing can keep us apart. I won't let it!" Tears filled both their eyes. Her lips were quivering as she leaned over and kissed him.

"I love you so much! What's going to happen to us now? I mean, won't there be an investigation?"

"Yes, but it won't affect you in any way. They will be out to nail me for wrecking the plane and for Lt. Keaton's death. But for now, I have to get back on my feet. The consequences will come soon enough."

"But Don, what about your career? Don't you care about that anymore?"

"Colonel Bates knows me too well to think the accident was entirely my fault. Frankly, I don't know why we stalled out. But inside I know that I should have recognized the stall coming. I'll live with this one for a long time."

"What do you think they will do to you?"

"Court-martial me, if they think it was my fault. They'll ground me or throw me out of the service." As they both looked at each other forlornly, a nurse entered the ward.

Addressing Jill she said, "I'm sorry, but Lt. Jennings needs to rest now."

"I'll be back later," Jill said as she squeezed his hand tightly. Forcing a smile, Don watched her limp down the long room. He stared at her curvaceous form until she was out of sight. He longed to hold her. A sick feeling came over him—he may never get that chance again.

Jill was headed back to her barracks. She wondered what she would tell her peers. She knew one thing—she would never disclose her true feelings for Don. She was relieved when she found the barracks deserted.

Meanwhile Colonel Bates shuffled through the papers on his desk, trying to find the accident forms. When he finally found them, he made up four sets—one for each member of the crew. He asked his orderly to deliver the forms with his instructions for them to be completed and returned to him by noon of the following day.

Bates didn't want Lt. Jennings to be court-martialed, but considering the facts, he knew Jennings would be found guilty of violating regulations. Since he was the squadron commander, he would have to make the final judgment. Now Bates had to address his most important decision; who would he select to sit on the review board? He thumbed through his list of flying officers and came up with three—Captain Short, Major Turner and Colonel Behnke. All were P-61 pilots, familiar with every characteristic of the plane that Jennings had crashed, and each had flown with Don, either as a check pilot or on a training mission back in the States. Bates felt he could trust these three to be fair and unbiased. He then selected a date for the board to convene and had his orderly deliver the notices to the officers.

Jill was preparing to return to the hospital when she received the accident form. She studied the questions. The more she contemplated her answers the more she became confused and worried. She folded the form, stuck it in her pocket and headed for the hospital. Jerry and Jordan were already with Don when she arrived. They needed Don's help in answering the questions too. The accident questions were very specific—the number in the crew, where they were positioned, the air speed, the weather, the possible reasons for the crash, etc. Jerry asked Don what he thought caused the crash.

"I firmly believe we stalled out, but I was watching the airspeed throughout the climb and I never saw it drop below the red line."

"Was it close?" Jordan asked.

"It was ten miles per hour above the red line, so when I felt the shudder I stayed on the rudders to avoid falling off into a spin," Don replied.

"But can we say we think the aircraft stalled out?" Jerry chimed in.

Jill said, "I don't know what you guys are talking about, but I'm sure its something they won't ask me about; discussion of what you were doing or what happened with the controls is something that I do not need to be part of. I am just going to check that box on the form."

Jerry added his general agreement with Jill.

"Let's take the other questions one at a time," Don suggested. "They will want to know about four people on a three-man crew airplane."

"Aside from the fact that four were aboard and that one was a woman will raise a few eyebrows," Jordan said firmly.

"I actually wrote Jill in as an observer on the flight. The Air Force can't object to that. The problem is the three-seat deal. Jerry, you shared your seat with Jordan. Regulations require everyone to have their own seat belt, harness and parachute. That's the rub!"

"But what was I assigned to observe?" Jill asked.

"You were looking for Japanese troops up on that mountain, just as Lt. Bond was there to do," Jerry pointed out. "So that's the whole story."

Don knew the story sounded plausible. And even though it wasn't exactly the way it happened, he hoped it would convince the review board.

All four marked their questionnaires accordingly. Upon completion, Jordan and Jerry lightened the conversation and tried to lift Don's morale with jokes and small talk.

The hospital ward was steaming hot with humidity—mimicking the tropical weather outside. Don was more than uncomfortable, and his spirits were beginning to dim. He worried about his friends' futures as well as his own, and wished the review board hearings were over. One thing was certain—this foursome had a firm conviction that their survival was meant for a purpose—to tie them together in a unique experience. No accident review board could take that away from them.

Jerry and Jordan shook Don's hand—insisting they had to go. They both knew Don wanted to talk to Jill alone.

"They're so thoughtful," Jill said as the twosome disappeared around the corner.

"Swell guys," Don added.

"Jill, no matter what happens at the hearing, I don't want you to take any of the blame. I talked you into coming along for a ride. I never dreamt it would end up the way it did."

"Don, I don't intend to say anything other than what we put on the form, if they call me to testify. We will all survive—just as we did the crash."

"Will you promise me that you won't hold it against me if I have to be separated from you for a short time?"

"I promise, and if we are separated, please promise me you will stay in touch with me, Don."

"You have my word on that Jill. Now stop worrying about all this and try to get some rest. You look beat!" Jill leaned over and kissed him. They parted as before, with caring eyes and aching hearts.

Lt. Colonel Behnke, Major Turner and Captain Short studied their accident questionnaires. They were able to come to a unanimous conclusion—that Lt. Don Jennings violated military flying regulations. He took an unauthorized person, Jill Harris, aboard his flight. The board also felt he had failed to take precautions when his flying speed slowed to a dangerous level. They placed full responsibility on him for the accident and for the subsequent injuries and death of an army officer. The board recommended Lt. Jennings be brought before a summary court-martial panel.

When Bates received this report, he studied it carefully. He had hoped they would have overlooked some of Jennings' errors. Don was one of the best pilots he had, and his fearlessness was an excellent quality for a combat flyer. Yet Bates knew that if he didn't get Jennings off the base quickly, he would have to bring him up on the charges the board had recommended. Bates liked Don too much to see him court-martialed, so he hastily made his way to the hospital to seek out Colonel Jason Bard, chief surgeon on staff.

"Colonel Bard, I need to get your opinion on Jennings. Is he strong enough to be shipped back to the mainland hospital tomorrow?" Colonel Bard pulled Don's medical record.

"It appears that he is stable, but he has fractured vertebrae. I think his body cast should keep him rigid enough to withstand the flight."

"Fine. Where do you want him sent in the States?"

"The best place would be March Field at Riverside, California. I'm sure you're familiar with it."

"Yes, I am. I've flown out of March many times. I'll arrange for his transportation and let you know. Meanwhile, I'd like to talk to Lt. Jennings and fill him in on the details."

"Very well Colonel Bates. We'll be ready when you are."

Exiting the staff office, Bates made his way to Don's ward. As he approached, he saw three people standing by Don's bedside. "Good morning," Bates said.

"Good morning Sir," Lt. Hurwitz replied as he stepped aside to let Bates move closer to Don's bed.

"Good morning, Colonel Bates," Don began. "Colonel, I know you know Lt. Hurwitz, but perhaps you don't know Sergeant Jill Harris and Lt.

Jordan Bond. They were on board when my plane went in."

"I'm glad to see you are in better shape than Lt. Jennings. I know you must have had a time of it up there."

Laughing nervously, Jill replied, "We'll be fine now that we're back safely. We sure do feel bad for Lt. Jennings."

"Yes, he's the one who took the brunt of it," Jerry interceded.

"Lt. Bond, I understand you saved the day for all of them by taking out the sniper."

"I'm just glad there was only one Jap soldier. I'm really sorry about Lt. Keaton, Sir."

"Yes, so am I. He was a good man."

Bates placed his hand on Don's cast. "This thing will be with you for a while I'm afraid."

"I guess," Don replied.

"Well, I have come to tell you that you'll be leaving for the States tomorrow. Your treatment will be continued at March Air Force Base Hospital in California. One more thing, you needn't worry about those accident forms; they won't go any further than my desk."

"I'm thankful for that, Colonel."

Bates then turned to Jerry. "There's no one I can assign you to, since my crews are already formed. You'll have to do some ground duty for now."

Jerry flinched. "Well Colonel, I guess I can manage somehow till things change."

"Lt. Bond you'll be flying Jennings back to the States, since you are with the transport command."

"I'll be happy to do that Sir. He's been a good friend to me."

"Sergeant Harris, I'm sure you will be rejoining your unit with your duties back in flight operations."

"Yes Sir."

"Additionally, Lieutenant Jennings, I wanted to reward that young native who saved your life. All I could find out came from the native who works in the mess hall, and it wasn't much," Bates added.

"What's his name Colonel? Where is he from?" Don wanted to know.

"Called himself Zainal. He came from one of the many Dani tribes, which are wide-spread in this area; we have no way of knowing which one," Bates replied. Then Bates politely wished them all well, shook their hands and departed.

The foursome heaved a sigh of relief that there would be no disciplinary action against them. But they now knew their close relationship would be severed with Don's immediate departure for the States. Jerry was the first to speak. "Do you believe this shit? He's grounding me!"

"It won't be for long," Don said, attempting to reassure him.

"Yeah, I'll be back flying when some bastard gets killed and leaves a spot open. Only trouble with that is, if the radar operator gets killed, the pilot most likely will be too!"

"They'll reassign you to a new ship, or alternate you with one of the existing crews that are waiting for those new P-61's," Don insisted.

Jill, holding back tears, told them she had some things she had to do and quietly left. Don knew how badly she was feeling. He wanted desperately to talk with her alone.

Jordan also decided to leave, to check operations and see what was on the transport schedule.

"I think I'll ask the Doc when I'm getting out of this place," Jerry muttered, as a wave of remorse swept over him. "Here I am feeling sorry for myself when you're the one in that damn hot body cast! I'm sorry for sounding like such a prick, Don."

"Forget it. Things will work out for the best. We just have to hang in there, Jerr."

"Thanks for being so understanding, buddy. Now you take it easy and I'll see you soon."

Later that evening Jill was ordered to report to her superior's office. "Yes, Major Barnes, you sent for me?"

"Sergeant Harris, we're transferring you to the base at Biak, simply to spare you any embarrassment over the accident. You could have been severely reprimanded for taking off on an unauthorized flight."

"So this is my punishment then?"

"I wouldn't call it that Sgt. Harris. Let's just say the transfer was requested because of a need for your operational talents on Biak."

"Have I been written up on my permanent records?"

"Not to my knowledge. I think you've learned a valuable lesson, and you've suffered enough. Don't take it so badly. Biak is a busy place, and I'm sure you'll find your duty there very satisfying. Now go back to your quarters and get some rest before tomorrow morning."

Extending her hand, Major Barnes shook Jill's hand gently, and with a motherly smile, wished her good luck on her new assignment.

"Thank you Major Barnes. I'll miss you." She saluted again and made her way out. Tears rolled down her cheeks. She felt the pain of loss—not only of her job but of the impending separation from Don. "How could her life get so screwed up so fast?" she asked herself.

Jill packed her duffle bag, then made her way back to Don's bedside. When he heard she was leaving for Biak, he agreed with Major Barnes and concluded she was being spared a great deal of heartache, and her military record would not be flawed.

Still, Jill felt she was being treated unfairly, but Don kept insisting that she was not, and that it was strictly a routine move. The military wanted to keep things from being blown out of proportion concerning the crash. Jill finally accepted his arguments and changed the subject.

"Don, when you get back to the States, will you be with your wife?"

"I don't know," he replied, knowing it was a lie.

"Will you write to me as soon as you can?"

"Of course. But don't fret if you don't hear from me right away. You know how long it takes mail to reach us out here."

"I'll never forget you, Don."

"Honey, remember what I told you. We'll be together again before too long. I love you. Hold onto our memories until then."

When it was time to go, they kissed long and tenderly. Then Jill straightened up, looked down at him and gave a sharp salute. "Good-bye Lieutenant."

Tears rolled down Don's cheeks. He would always remember her, and one day, somewhere, somehow, he knew he would find a way back to her.

In the morning, Jordan made his way to the flight line with his copilot to board the C-47 that would carry Don and several other patients to the States. Jordan had notified Jerry of his departure time. Jerry was waiting when the ambulances arrived with the evacuees. Jerry walked alongside Don as he was carried to the plane.

A second C-47 transport was parked nearby, and as Don and the other patients were loaded aboard the hospital transport, a jeep drove up carrying Jill Harris and three other military personnel. They quickly boarded the adjacent transport.

Jerry bid Don and Jordan farewell and backed away, as an Army nurse closed the aircraft door.

The engines were started and soon Jordan's ship was taxing out behind the plane carrying Jill Harris.

Jerry watched the transports climb gracefully away, becoming mere dots in the sky. And he was alone.

Twelve

The air was rough and storm clouds billowed ahead. One hour into his flight, Jordan set his magnetic compass heading toward Guam. Lt. Harry Welsh, his co-pilot, seemed pre-occupied with getting a fix from the radio operator. Suddenly he shouted, "I'm picking up a May Day!"

"What frequency?"

"I'm trying to determine…there, I have it! 22.9 mega hertz." Jordan switched from his intercom to the radio frequency.

"May Day, May Day! This is Air Force two-niner-zero. My engines are out and we're going down!"

"Get his position," Jordan said to Welsh.

"Aircraft in distress, can you give a position? Over."

"Roger, we are approximately one hundred miles southeast of Biak Island. We're at five thousand and descending through solid overcast. Over."

"Christ! Two-niner-zero might be Colonel Bates!" Jordan cried out.

"Is Colonel Bates on board your aircraft? Over."

"That's affirmative. This is Colonel Bates. Over."

"Roger, Colonel Bates. We'll break and advise the base of your position. Keep transmitting, and keep your mike open so they can get an accurate fix on your position," Jordan shouted.

"Roger, we'll prepare to ditch if no beaches are below when we break through this overcast."

Then there was silence. Continued efforts to contact Bates met with failure. Jordan knew their only hope would have to come from Biak. He radioed Biak and was informed they had already plotted a fix on the position of the stricken C-47.

Jordan was distraught. "They've gone in! Colonel Bates and Jill Harris are on that ship! Keep monitoring that frequency to see if anyone from Biak gets out there."

"Yes Sir!"

Jordan, unable to assist and feeling helpless, held his course for Guam and believed that Biak would locate the downed craft. He didn't have the heart to inform Don Jennings of what had happened.

He would wait until he learned more, perhaps when he reached Guam. Turning over the controls to Lt. Welsh, Jordan headed aft to check on his passengers. Everyone was asleep except Don. He hadn't slept since he parted from Jill.

"How's it going, Don?"

"I guess I'll survive."

"Can I get you anything?"

"Yeah; how about a new back!"

Jordan gave a faint smile.

"Kidding aside, how's it going up there in the cockpit—anything exciting?"

"We have a good tail wind and should make Guam ahead of our ETA."

"Thanks for checking on me, Tuskegee. I'm okay."

Jordan felt rotten for not telling Don about the distress call from Bates, but he knew it was best to hold off—he might hear better news when they reach Guam.

Making his way back to the cockpit, he questioned his co-pilot; "Anything on Colonel Bates?"

"Nothing yet."

"How's our ground speed?"

"With this tail wind, we're really sailing. We should be at Guam in about two hours."

"Great! Let's hope the weather holds."

Jordan landed at Guam thirty minutes ahead of his ETA, and headed directly to the operation's office. He found an Air Force intelligence officer who told him that a Guam bomber crew had also heard the distress call. Jordan urged the officer to contact Biak to see if their search craft had located the C-47, and the officer agreed to try. In the meantime, Jordan went back to the flight line to get his aircraft refueled. When Jordan returned to operations, the intelligence officer informed him that Air Force two-niner-zero was not found. They presumed it had sunk somewhere south of Biak Island and there were no signs of survivors. The crew was officially listed as missing.

Concealing his feelings of sadness, Jordan returned to his plane to begin the next leg of his journey. He decided to spare Don the news and focused on getting his injured people back to the mainland. As he passed Don's cot, Don was sound asleep and Jordan muttered to himself, "Why do such bad things have to happen to such good people?"

The long flight from Guam to Hawaii was uneventful. Jordan's passengers needed a respite from the long, bumpy ride and the crew had to sleep, so they would lay over here for the night. And there would be quiet, private time, appropriate for completing an unpleasant task. Jordan mustered up his courage and went to talk to Don. "Don, I have some bad news to tell you."

"Don't tell me they're going to make us stay here a couple of days."

"Nothing like that. It's far more serious." Now Don could see Jordan's face, and hear in his voice, that this was a painfully life-changing matter.

"I'm afraid—oh hell, I don't know any other way to break it to you! Jill was on board a plane that went down on a flight to Biak."

"How do you know that?"

"We heard the distress call. They went down about one hundred miles south of Biak. Both engines quit on 'em. Search and rescue believes the plane sank. The crew is listed as missing."

"How can you be sure?"

"I talked with intelligence in Guam. They confirmed it with Biak."

Don closed his eyes—seeing before him only his last image of Jill. He was unable to talk further, and in an almost inaudible voice he asked to be alone. Jordan patted his arm and hesitated, then with bowed head he left Don's side. Don lay motionless, questioning himself; "Why did I make this happen? Is this my punishment for being in love with two women at the same time? Was this meant to keep Jill and me apart forever?" He prayed silently to God to spare Jill—to let her make it to safety somewhere. He pleaded over and over again, "Please God let her live! She is too young to die!"

He prayed for hours but found no reassurance. God didn't answer him. He thought that maybe this is how Christ must have felt as he hung on the cross. Christ too, had asked God to take this cup from him, to spare him this agony. But Christ didn't find an answer until he gave up his spirit totally to God. The answer was the resurrection.

Don was unable to sleep, and by morning he was spent. The plaster cast around his body reeked of sweat, and his spirit was filled with despair. But through it all, he just couldn't conceive of Jill's demise.

The next two days were spent in relative silence by both Don and Jordan. When their plane landed at March Field, Jordan knew his association with Don would now end. He made sure Don was secure in his hospital bed and assured him he would keep in touch. And then he was gone.

Don was dizzy with the sudden changes in his career and his life. He realized that he was now back in California, where he had a wife, but he was feeling too ashamed to contact her. Her hero had shipped out to fight the enemy, and now he was back wrapped in a cast—never having had a chance to engage the enemy. He would hold off calling Betty until he had more information about his length of stay at this hospital. But he knew that his "more information" thing was just an excuse; what he really needed was more time to get over his sad feelings about Jill before he faced Betty.

What Don did not know was that Betty had been notified of his injuries, she knew where he was being sent and she was already on her way. So the morning following his arrival, Betty, armed with a small vase of fresh flowers, quietly walked into his hospital room. She stopped just a couple of steps inside the door, caught a breath, and then went quickly to Don's side.

Don, wide-eyed with surprise, raised his arms in an attempt to hug her. After a long moment Don broke the tearful silence. "You're more beautiful than ever," he whispered. Her face was radiant, and the smell of her hair and the touch of her lips brought back all the reminders of how much he really loved her.

"I'm sorry I didn't call you, honey, I was too ashamed. I'm nothing now. I didn't want you to see me like this."

"Oh Don! How foolish! If you knew how much I missed you, you would never think like that! You can't get rid of me that easily! You'll be back on your feet in no time. I know how strong-willed you are."

He knew everything she said was true. He would fight back fast, and he would do it even quicker now that he had Betty's support.

"Honey, I know you're right. It's just that I felt like such a failure. I didn't want to face you before I got out of this cast." He knew, in his heart, he had deceived her. One day he would tell her everything, but for now he couldn't bring himself to hurt her.

Before her visit ended, Betty proposed that she get a job in nearby Riverside, so as to be near him every day throughout his recuperation. Her pronouncement relieved Don of the fears he had been harboring. She loved him for who he was inside.

After six weeks, Don's cast was removed and he began a six-week therapy program. X-rays had revealed that his vertebrae had healed. All the while, Betty's daily visits were a great morale booster, and she was proud of Don's perseverance to be able to walk again. Finally the day came when he was pronounced fit for duty. When his hospital discharge orders came, he studied them carefully. He was being assigned temporarily to ground duty with the Air Force Intelligence at Mather Field near Sacramento.

Disappointed that he was not being restored to flight status, Don pressed for flight duty reinstatement. The flight surgeon, however, would not seriously consider his request and stressed to Don that the G-forces would affect, and perhaps prevent, his full permanent recovery.

Don immediately started intelligence school classes, and he trained diligently. Deep inside, however, he was miserable. His back ached from sitting for long periods in the classroom; Betty's invaluable day-to-day support was his driving force.

Thirteen

Colonel Bates was at the controls of the lumbering C-47 transport heading for Biak Island. Jill sat alone in a bucket seat near the huge rear door, sadly reliving the events that had torn Don away from her. Suddenly the plane bounced. She pulled her seatbelt tighter. The plane climbed out of the rough air, and all was peaceful again, but not for long. Without warning, the plane's left engine backfired and died!

Bates quickly feathered the prop on the dead engine and trimmed the ship for level flight. He cursed the engine as he tried to restart it. Then the unthinkable happened, the right engine failed!

Bates remained calm and quickly established a normal glide through the heavy overcast below.

His copilot, Lieutenant Bill Rankin, frantically radioed May Day emergency distress calls in hopes of alerting someone who could initiate land and sea rescue operations. Crew Chief Sergeant George Troxell dashed out of the cockpit into the cabin and shouted to Jill to prepare for a crash landing. "Don't inflate your life vest until we're outside the aircraft Sergeant!" Troxell yelled. They both braced themselves for the impact.

Within minutes the plane splashed into the ocean, and it did so without causing injury or trauma to any of the occupants. Bates had somehow been able to keep the nose up and to greatly slow the craft before splash down. Bates and Rankin entered the cabin and headed toward the rear of the aircraft and assisted Troxell in opening the wide door. After pulling the raft's inflation pin, the three men tossed the raft out the door. Jill jumped into the raft, followed by the others. Bates and Troxell grabbed the oars and began paddling away from the plane as it sank from sight.

Catching her breath, Jill scanned the sea around her and pointed as she yelled, "I think I see land over there!" The others agreed. They steered the raft toward the faint outline on the horizon. The sky was darkening with an approaching rainsquall and the ocean swells were mounting. The two men paddled vigorously trying to make land before the squall hit. But within minutes they were being pounded relentlessly by wind and rain. The storm raged over them for nearly half an hour as they held on to each other and to the perimeter rope to avoid being swept overboard. Then, as quickly as it had appeared, the storm subsided and the once angry sea became surprisingly calm and peaceful.

"Is everyone okay?" Bates asked.

Drenched from head to toe, Jill jokingly said she could use some dry clothes.

"I'd prefer the sight of a rescue plane," Lt. Rankin quipped.

"They're bound to spot us now that the squall is past," Troxell reassured.

"We can't count on it so let's keep paddling. That island can't be more than a mile away," Bates concluded.

Troxell located the emergency signaling radio stored in the raft, inflated the balloon that hoisted the radio's antenna and began cranking the handle, sending out continuous S.O.S. signals.

"Did you pocket your navigational chart Lt. Rankin?" Bates asked.

"Yes, but it's soaked."

Sgt. Troxell kept the crank handle turning, and Jill kept her eyes peeled on the island. She was never fond of the sea. Its vastness and endless waves gave her a feeling of helplessness. She felt she was now again being tested for her strength and convictions as an independent woman—striving to be equal with her male counterparts. Inwardly she longed to be back in Don's arms and away from this nightmare.

Then Jill realized they were about to reach land as they began to dip and sway in the gentle breaking waves approaching the island beach. Bates jumped into the shallow water and held the raft steady while the others climbed out. Together they dragged the raft ashore and then surveyed their surroundings. They were soon relieved to discover that the island was inhabited, when they saw footprints in the sand. They assumed the prints were made by natives.

The four sat down to rest and Bates praised the trio for working together to make it safely ashore. "We'll get off this island once a rescue plane spots us." Jill sensed that he was trying to boost their morale rather than saying what he was really thinking. Not a single plane had been seen or heard after the weather cleared. Sgt. Troxell volunteered to explore the island to see if he could make contact with the natives, but Bates vetoed the idea. "We'd better wait a few hours. Let's stay together and see if the natives come to us. If they aren't friendly, they'd be quick to do away with you if you were alone. There's strength in numbers."

"Perhaps we could take these wet clothes off and try to dry them out before the sun gets too low," Rankin suggested. They all agreed. Soon they were all down to their underwear. They laid their clothes on the beach and sat down in a circle. Jill was somewhat embarrassed with this situation. All the men assured her they would not look at her until she was dressed again, and it took less than fifteen minutes for the clothes to dry in the hot sun.

Troxell suggested they look for some food before dark. They set out for the trees not far from shore, and Jill spotted bananas. Troxell climbed the tree and dropped a bunch to the ground. The bananas were ripe and tasty and quickly devoured.

Lt. Rankin had dried the aeronautical chart in the sun, and now he and Bates scanned it closely. Bates estimated that they had been about a hundred miles south of Biak Island when his engine quit. Unfortunately, there were a dozen islands on the chart that were within a fifty-mile radius of Biak. None of the islands were named. They appeared to be ten miles east of the New Guinea coastline.

"I'm not exactly sure where we are. My hunch is we are here at this tiny island." He pointed to a small spot on the map. "If we find the natives they can get us to Yapen Island. Then we wouldn't be too far from Biak, located here to the northwest."

Jill was not encouraged by what she was hearing. She kept her feelings to herself and joined the others in exploring the island. The warm sun filtered through the trees to illuminate clusters of strange, beautiful flowers and plants, and brightly colored exotic birds were everywhere. The tropical paradise almost made Jill forget their plight, as the island's tranquil beauty gave her a new zest for life. But she was called back to reality with Colonel Bates's abrupt command to halt.

At first Jill didn't understand the concern in Bates's voice, as she saw only more paradise all around her. Then something chilling began to appear to her in the green puzzle of jungle. Directly in front of them stood a group of dark-skinned natives, dressed only in a few leaves that covered their private parts. They had large bone rings piercing their noses. Their faces were painted white and their attitude unfriendly, as they pointed spears at the Americans. Bates forced a smile—the only universal language he knew. The leader finally moved and gestured the group to lower their spears. Jill quickly pleaded with Bates to allow her to communicate with them.

"Very well Sgt. Harris; maybe you can help our cause. But you are probably the first white woman they have ever seen, and I don't know if that is good or bad." Jill motioned for the chieftain and the others to sit down with them. Surprisingly he accepted and the natives formed a circle around the four Americans. Jill offered them a banana. The chief laughingly took the banana and held it up for the others to see. The natives broke into wild laughter.

"Here, give them my watch," Troxell ordered. Jill showed the watch to the chieftain. She held it to his ear. An astonished look came over his face as he examined the timepiece. Jill put it on his wrist and fastened it. With a broad smile he raised his arm to show the others. To them it was a bracelet of rare beauty. As a final gesture, Jill removed her high school ring and put it on the little finger of the chieftain. The chieftain smiled broadly again, as Jill stared at a mouth filled with snaggled, decayed teeth. While he displayed his pot-holed enamel, the chieftain removed the bone necklace from around his neck and handed it to Jill. She put it over her neck in a gesture of gratitude. All of the natives jumped to their feet and began to dance about. Jill gestured to the others to join them in the tribal dance. The ritual finally ended with the natives embracing the Americans. Jill was proud of herself and could feel the good relationship she had developed with the natives. Her mind flashed back to her schoolgirl days when she sat in the movie theaters watching "Tarzan of the Apes." Now if she could only convey to these new friends where they must go, but before she could think of what she should do next, the tribal chief motioned for the four to follow him. The mixed procession moved along for about half an hour. Then the chief motioned for the Americans to sit down. He fixed his gaze upon a small clearing and sat motionless. In a few minutes, a fierce-looking native dressed in colored feathers and carrying a large spear, burst into the clearing. He shouted and ranted angrily for several minutes.

When the ranting finally ended, the chief motioned for the foursome to rise. Several of the natives bound their hands behind their backs. The foursome marched off, tied to each other by one continuous cord of twine with the guardsmen honed in close beside them. They traveled for over an hour when they broke through a clearing into a village. There were at least fifty thatched huts encircling the area in an uneven pattern. Women and children stopped what they were doing and stared inquisitively at them. A fire burned brightly in the center of the village. The march ended in front of one of the larger huts and the four were ushered inside where they were left alone.

"I think our hosts are trying to decide what to do with us," Bates said.

"The chief knows we aren't here to harm them. Jill's breakthrough established that," Lt. Rankin added.

"I'm not sure about anything. The natives were pretty friendly. It's that weirdo who harassed the chief that we need to be concerned about," Jill offered.

"I agree. We should try to negotiate with the chief since he is the only one who can get us out of this mess. When they return, maybe you can talk with the chief again Jill," Bates suggested.

They all discussed what they could give the chief that would catch his eye. The only thing they could come up with was a pair of silver wings that Lt. Rankin was wearing on his shirt. While they were discussing strategy, the angry native that Jill called "weirdo" entered the hut. He had shed his wardress and stood before them with a more peaceful but intense stare. Without speaking, he sat down in the midst of them, as the chief entered along with two other natives—a male and a female.

The chief raised his hand as though calling the meeting to order. He gestured to the native female to speak. To their surprise, she spoke in broken English and addressed her remarks to Jill.

"My people want to know why you here."

"We are Americans. We were flying in an airplane and we crashed in the ocean. We are trying to return to Biak Island. Do you know where that is?"

The native interpreted Jill's remarks to the Chief. The chief spoke a few words, and the interpreter addressed Jill again. "My chief want to know if you have chief?"

Jill pointed to Colonel Bates. Bates smiled and raised his hand as if to greet them in a leadership fashion. He then turned to the interpreter and asked her the position of the native who first came into the hut ahead of them.

"He medicine man. He tell chief all things. He tell chief not get close to you. Your skin white so you sick. He no want our people get sick like you."

The four captors felt relieved at what she had said.

"But you know we are not sick since you must have learned English from white people," Jill pressed.

"I taken from my island by this tribe's warriors. I learned English from traders before. These native know nothing of white man. Medicine man say kill you. Chief listen to me when I tell him you make no mean. He tell medicine man and that why he here. He want learn more. I afraid for you."

Bates said, "This woman must convince them that all we want is to reach Biak Island." He asked Jill to try to persuade the interpreter.

"May I ask your name?"

"I Tiara."

"Tiara, my name is Jill. We only want to get to Biak Island. Do you know where that is?"

"No, I not heard it."

"What is this island called?"

"It is Kawkek. It mean turtle."

Bates asked Rankin for the map. His eyes finally settled on an island called Kaurudu because it was shaped like a turtle. He asked Tiara if she knew where Samberbaba was.

Tiara smiled and answered. "My people come from there. I not go there but it near setting sun and two day passing from here."

Bates' eyes brightened.

Looking at Tiara and tearing up, Jill took her hand and cupped it in her own. "Yes we need your help to get to Samberbaba. Can you help us?"

"If chief agree, I take you there." Tiara made a passionate plea to the chief for the release of the Americans. The chief listened and then stood up and motioned for the other natives to follow him.

"They apparently have gone to take up the matter with others. We just have to play their game," Bates spoke out.

"What do you know about Samberbaba?" Jill asked.

"Just that it lies south of Biak and is one of the larger islands in the chain. The natives are more civilized, I'm told since they are closer to Biak where many of our troops have landed. It is about fifty miles from here."

After an hour passed, Tiara returned tearfully to announce that the chief would not release them. The council was debating as to how to kill them.

Tiara waited till the guards left the prisoners, who were still bound in the hut. She quickly cut their ties and told them to follow her. Under the cover of darkness, they made their way out of the village, through the jungle and after two hours arrived on the beach on the west side of the island. Two young native boys were waiting for them. They were Tiara's sons. The boys would man the long boat that would take them off the island. Tiara remained behind so she would not be accused of assisting in their escape.

The young boys never stopped paddling and the Americans marveled at their strength and endurance. Soon they were ashore where the boys hid the boat in a cove. They motioned for the four to follow them into the jungle.

Dawn was breaking when the boys stopped. The mountains were just before them. They would have to climb the range. After an exhausting eight hours, they had climbed over the mountains and were standing on a sandy beach. The boys built a fire to draw attention to their location. When morning came, so did the boat people from across the land to the west. The leader was a strong man who stood nearly seven feet tall. His speech was a mixture that included broken English.

Colonel Bates gestured and asked if he knew of Biak. The man smiled and nodded.

"Many birds fly from there everyday."

"Do you mean machine birds?"

The leader nodded.

Soon Jill and Bates were aboard one of the long boats while Troxell and Rankin climbed aboard the second boat. None of them knew how far they had to travel to their destination. Jill's eyes filled with tears as she looked back at the two young boys on the beach. She raised her hand and waved to them. They waved back until they were no longer in her sight.

Fourteen

$\mathcal{B}$ack at Capur, Jerry Hurwitz learned that Colonel Bates and his crew were reported missing on the downed flight to Biak. Jerry's time in New Guinea was turning into a nightmare. With Bates gone as squadron commander, Jerry now wondered if he would ever be assigned to another P-61 crew. Weeks went by without a flying assignment, and Jerry was miserable. He suffered humiliation from the other radar operators who nicknamed him "the de-winged OR." At other times he would feel the "just kidding" sting of anti-Semitism, "Hey, Jew Boy without your screw-up pilot, Jennings." Sometimes he almost wished he had died in the crash on the mountain; but most of all, he longed to be assigned to a crew.

Finally, when a Major Mel (Yank) Yankovich arrived in the squadron accompanied by an unhealthy radar operator, Jerry was assigned, if only temporarily, to fill in. They flew night missions, known to be long and tiresome, searching for seemingly non-existent enemy aircraft. But on their fifth mission, life became exciting when Jerry spotted a bogie as they flew north of Iwo Jima.

"Got one on the scope," Jerry called to Yank. "He's twenty miles north at twelve o'clock."

"Roger," Yank replied, sounding almost like a gleeful schoolboy.

As they flew through the night sky, Jerry kept his eyes on the enlarging blip, which began a wide turn. "He's turning left. Turn 270 degrees, Major."

Yank adjusted course to stay on a beeline toward the target. The plane ahead seemed to be slowing down, and it meandered aimlessly. Then the blip became the center dot on the scope.

"I have him in sight!" Yank shouted "…. Jesus, it has four engines! It's a B-29! What the hell is he doing out here?…. I'm going to pull up alongside him and see what's up."

As he flew alongside the lumbering bomber he could see that the pilot was slouched over in the cockpit. "The pilot is hurt. I'm going to check out the co-pilot," Yank yelled. He dropped back, flew under the Super Fortress and came up on its right side to see a gaping hole in the fuselage.

"See if you can raise that guy on guarded emergency frequency, Jerry."

Jerry called for the B-29 to acknowledge.

"This is Seven-zero-zero. We're in a heap of trouble out here," came the reply.

"Seven-zero-zero, we're right beside you. Christ, it looks like you're installing patio doors. What's your status?" Yank asked.

"My pilot's dead. We took a cannon blast before we reached the target. I'm half blinded from shrapnel. My electrical and hydraulic systems are out; I can't see a damn thing in this cockpit, and our navigator can't read his instruments either. We don't know where the hell we are. We're trying to get back to Saipan. Over."

"Roger, Seven-zero-zero. Can you see us beside you?"

"Barely."

"Okay. Try to follow me; we'll get you to Iwo," Yank assured him.

"Get Iwo, Jerry; tell them we have an emergency. We'll try to lead these guys in." "Iwo this is Bravo-Victor-Two-Niner-Niner. We are in a P-61 night fighter trying to assist a B-29 in trouble up here. Over."

"Bravo-Victor-Two-Niner-Niner. What is his status? Over."

Calling back to the stricken bomber, Yank asked how many crewmen were still alive.

"Ten of us."

"How much fuel do you have?"

"Should have plenty since we didn't make it to the target. Our bombs are still armed too!"

Iwo station replied to Jerry's call and when told of the situation, insisted there was no way the co-pilot could safely land the aircraft without instruments or hydraulics. The crew would have to bail out over the field.

Given the orders, the courageous young co-pilot passed the word back to the crew to get ready to bail out. Eventually the B-29 was successfully guided in and ready to pass over the landing strip at one thousand feet. Yank gave them the order to jump. Jerry saw ten chutes blossom below as Yank pulled up and away from the wobbly bomber.

"Aircraft assisting the B-29. We have a direct order to pass you," came the voice from the ground.

"Roger, Iwo. Go ahead."

"Destroy the B-29 as soon as it gets out over the sea. Repeat, shoot down that airplane!"

"Roger," Yank acknowledged. "Jerry, did you hear that?"

"Major, I heard it. That co-pilot must have set it on auto pilot; it's headed south now.... out to sea again."

The widest, longest, biggest, fastest bomber ever made, carrying a dead U.S. pilot and ten tons of bombs, had now become their target! With mixed feelings, they fired their twenty millimeter cannon and watched the tracers streak toward the giant bomber. Many of the shots appeared to hit the bomber directly on the right wing engine nacelles. The bomber flew on. Yank dove past the plane, circled and came in for another shot from the front. Every tracer appeared to strike it's intended target, but they failed to blow the huge bomber out of the sky—in fact they seemed to have no effect other than to cause the craft to start a slow turn.

"What the hell is holding that bastard up?" Yank hollered.

"I don't know, Major, but after that last burst she's making a wide turn and it looks like her course will take her right back toward Iwo!"

Swinging around to come in from a different angle on the side, Yank fired away with both cannon and fifty calibers. This time as the shells penetrated the bomber, a bright flash rose from the inboard engine, and the plane exploded in a mass of flames. They watched the broken ship fall from the sky. Another huge explosion of ten tons of bombs followed as the plane hit the water.

After reporting their success to Iwo, Major Yankovich and Lieutenant Hurwitz were saddened and somewhat embarrassed that they had shot down one of America's precious premier war machines— and with the pilot still inside. With strong and confused emotions, they returned to their base in silence.

Back at the base it became a reflective time for Jerry. Jerry knew Major Yankovich was generally a skillful pilot, but it was also apparent to him that Yank had a drinking problem; a problem that was getting out of hand. After each mission Yank would belt down scotch and soda until he was drunk. As their missions multiplied, so did his drinking. Because he was a junior ranked officer, Jerry could not easily address Yank's dangerous habit, and he was frustrated as he watched it get worse.

Before Jerry could figure out a way to attenuate Yank's drinking problem, Yank's regular OR returned to active duty, and Jerry was grounded once again. This time Jerry didn't really mind. He was not only frustrated with Yank, but he was tired and was ready for some rest and relaxation. Jerry found an R&R flight scheduled for Sydney posted on the bulletin board; he signed on. To his surprise, Major Yankovich was also granted leave, and was assigned to pilot the C-47 transport for the trip. What was less surprising, when Jerry showed up for the flight, was that he climbed into the cockpit to pilot Jerry and the twenty-three other servicemen to Sidney. Yank was still red-eyed from a hangover. On take-off, the landing gear came up just as the left engine lost power. The plane veered sharply to the left and lost altitude. Jerry looked out the window to see the wing dip, and he knew they were going to crash. Yank tried to climb, skipped over a B-17 bomber bunkered in a dugout area, but then caught the roof of a hangar and burst into flames! Four hours later Jerry was beginning his R&R, but his would be right there in the base hospital. Miraculously, every man aboard was able to get out of the burning craft but most suffered second and third degree burns. Jerry's arm was badly burned.

Major Yankovich escaped uninjured. Two weeks later, he was found directing traffic on the streets of Sydney—stark naked and drunk! Yank had made it to Sidney only to have the war and his drinking finally take its toll on him, and end his career. The incident reflected on Jerry too. Squadron crewmen began hinting that "the Jew boy drove the old man to drink!" With that, Jerry asked for a transfer to the Lingayen Gulf squadron in northwest Luzon. But not much changed when he got to Lingayen. Jerry spent the remainder of the war as a "ground-pounding officer" doing menial duties and trying to forget the crash with Don Jennings that destroyed his military flight career.

Fifteen

fter a year of ground duty, Don
Jennings was given the bad news that
he would never be returned to flight
status in the Air Force. Disappointed to the point of
near depression, and bored with his military
assignment, Don resigned his commission and
returned to civilian life to seek a career as a
commercial pilot. He and Betty took up residence in
the San Fernando Valley and began their married
life anew.

Don drug out his military log book and
headed off to the Civil Aeronautics Authority office
in nearby L.A. He knew he was well qualified to
receive his commercial pilot's license. And sure
enough, he left the CAA office clutching the

cherished certificate. Don had only one major goal in mind as he drove directly to the offices of a small feeder airline based out of Van Nuys. With high hopes of immediately beginning his career in civil aviation, he was pleased to find that they were not just interested; they obviously wanted to offer him a position that very day. But to his surprise, he was told he would have to start out as a co-pilot in this small commuter line. The airport was conveniently close to his home, and he was confident that he could easily work his way up to first pilot, so Don accepted the job on the spot. Time passed quickly that year, and Don's Air Force training paid off; before a year was up, he was a Captain, seated in the left seat of the cockpit. And when the war at long last ended, the airline industry expanded. Don took an opportunity to earn a four-engine pilot rating in hopes of moving up to a major airline.

Meanwhile, Betty devoted her time to being the homemaker she had always longed to be. While Don harbored feelings of regret over his failed combat days in the service, he hid these feelings from Betty and wanted only to make their marriage a happy one. As Don's salary increased, and they were settled comfortably in their new surroundings, they appreciated how good life had become. They were in the prime of their lives and were realizing the American dream; and both agreed it was time to start a family. In anticipation of starting their perfect family, Don insisted that Betty get a complete physical exam, and she happily consented. But the outcome was disturbing—a small lump was found in Betty's right breast. The doctor told her it was a very tiny mass and not to worry about it for the time being. But their plans for starting a family were put on hold.

Betty relied on the doctor's opinion and went about her daily life almost just as before, but her disposition was subtly more reserved. She could not overlook the supposedly insignificant lump on her breast. Inside she felt something wasn't right and she would not be content until the lump was gone from her body. Several months passed and the lump in her breast increased in size. Now deeply concerned, Betty returned to her physician for another consultation. The doctor immediately took a biopsy. When the lab reports came back, it showed the mass was malignant! Betty was immediately scheduled for a mastectomy.

Don was angry that the doctor hadn't taken a biopsy of the lump when he had discovered it months ago, and he urged Betty to change doctors. She refused—indicating she had faith in this doctor because of his reputation as one of the best surgeons in the area. Moreover, he assured her that he could do a non-radical mastectomy—a less invasive form of breast surgery—and she would be fine. Betty secretly was afraid that another surgeon might prefer something more aggressive.

The removal of her breast and the chemotherapy treatments afterward were a trying experience for Betty. When her surgery healed and the "chemo" treatments ended, she opted to have reconstructive surgery. Emerging from the surgery beautifully reshaped and with a rekindled spirit, Betty finally returned to her normal self and developed a new zest for life and a heightened sensitivity for the needs and concerns of her friends and others. Betty became an inspiration to all who knew her.

Don's career blossomed as he became captain of one of the industry's streamlined, four-engine passenger airliners, the Lockheed Constellation, on continental routes. The huge star liner with its pressurized cabin, carrying 64-81 passengers was the pinnacle of propeller airline design, conceived by famed plane builder Howard Hughes and was known in flying circles as the "Connie." Its graceful lines and its near 100-foot long fuselage with a wingspan of 123 feet made it one of the most beautiful planes ever built. Don loved its cruising speeds at nearly 300 knots and its long range of 4,300 miles. The tripletail design and its porpoise-like nose made it the king of the airline industry. And Don's time at the controls of this magnificent airplane was more pleasure than work.

On his days off, he and Betty spent their time playing golf, dining at fine restaurants and traveling on long vacations. Their lives could not have been happier until the unexpected happened. Two years after she was pronounced free of cancer, a routine annual examination disclosed the disease had surfaced in the lymph nodes in her neck. Her oncologist elected to treat her with radiation. The cancerous cells disappeared, but a month later her right arm began to swell. Further tests showed the disease had spread to her lung and she was admitted to the hospital and a lung aspiration was performed immediately. When she awoke from the procedure, Don and the surgeon were at her side. Betty looked at them with an angelic smile, then looked directly at the doctor and asked softly, "How long do I have?"

The surgeon hesitated briefly and replied, "Six months or so."

Betty seemed to know he was not telling her the truth. She squeezed Don's hand, closed her eyes and fell back to sleep. Don kept a constant vigil at her bedside for hours and during the night, she sat up in bed, and as Don held her in his arms, she gasped a last breath and was gone.

Deeply depressed and guilt-ridden, Don's faith in the Almighty was tested once more. The two loves of his life had been taken away from him. He felt empty and alone.

Sixteen

*D*on's grief lingered for months and he hid his feelings by taking as many flights as the company would allow. To pass his off hours, he took up photography as a hobby. His hobby became his passion, so much so that he began displaying his work at local art shows.

Three years passed and his reputation as "Ansel Adams in the sky," was beginning to be publicized nationally. He arranged his flight schedules to coincide to his art show schedule, always refusing to give up his love of flying.

Often he chose show dates that would occur at the end of a run where he had a lay over before his return flight. On one such schedule he chose a show in Detroit. The show promotion announced that Don would make a personal appearance.

Don had checked into the Hilton Hotel. He tossed his bags on a chair, shed his tie and shirt and stretched out on the bed to relax when the phone rang.

"Damn," he muttered to himself. Picking up the phone he tried not to show his irritability and uttered a cordial greeting. A woman's voice penetrated his ear with a pleasant response.

"I hope I'm not disturbing you Mr. Jennings. Am I?"

"May I ask who is calling?"

"Well, I'd rather not say just yet. I would be embarrassed if you aren't the person I think you are. So, can you tell me if you have ever served in the Air Force?"

"Yes, during the war."

After a long silence, the woman continued. "Did you serve in the South Pacific Theatre?"

"Well, yes I did."

"Were you with a Night Fighter Squadron?"

"That's right, I was, for a time, that is. How do you know all of this about me? Just who are you?"

"We knew each other very well a long time ago. Don, I'm Jill Harris."

Don's heart skipped a beat. "Jill Harris! Is this a joke? I thought Jill was dead!"

"No, I'm really not; rumors of my death are greatly exaggerated," she replied gleefully.

"Jill! Why didn't you get in touch with me before now?" Don pressed.

"Let's talk about all that when we see each other. I mean, would you like to get together? I'm just a few doors down from your hotel. Would you mind if I came over? Perhaps we could have dinner."

Don hesitated for a moment, wondering if this was a hoax or some autograph seeker. But he knew that voice was Jill.

"That would be wonderful! I'll be in the lobby to meet you in twenty minutes."

"Great, I'll be there."

Don was stunned. He could hardly believe, after twelve years, that Jill was actually alive. He composed himself, slipped his shirt back on and grabbed his sport coat.

As he waited for Jill in the lobby, his mind raced. What would she look like? Would he recognize her when she came in? He tried to keep calm. Shortly he felt a tug at his coat. Turning around, he faced a beautiful woman whom he recognized instantly. It was Jill. Her face was radiant. He would have known her anywhere.

"Hi," she said.

"Jill, you look wonderful! You haven't changed a bit!"

"And neither have you!"

He reached for her hand and held it tightly. He held her at arms length. His eyes scanned her from head to toe. She was wearing a gorgeous black and white dress with a gold necklace. "Let's get out of here," he said.

"I'm sure there must be a good restaurant close by."

In a few minutes they settled into a corner table at a small French restaurant just a block from the hotel. Don gazed at her again with the look of a young man on his first date. He hardly knew how to begin a conversation. Finally he asked, "How did you know I was here?"

"I read about you in the newspaper. You are somewhat of a celebrity in the photography world."

"No, not really. I've had just a few things published. I'm so glad you caught the article! But tell me, what happened back there in New Guinea? I'm dying of curiosity. I was told you were lost at sea."

"We were lost at sea for some time. We made our way back to Biak with the help of some friendly natives. After that, we went back to our duties and that was the end of it. I knew you had gone back to the States and your wife. I just tried to get you out of my mind and focus on my career."

"Jill, I meant to tell you about my wife. You must believe that."

"It doesn't matter Don. Things couldn't have worked out between us. I'm not a home-wrecker and I still don't want to interfere in your married life. I just wanted to see you again."

"Jill, my wife died three years ago. I've been alone ever since. I haven't even had a date."

"I'm so sorry. I had no idea."

"Thanks Jill. So what have you been doing all these years?"

"After the war I came back to Detroit and started college. I studied, it felt like forever, and earned my BS and Master's degrees. I have a position in hospital administration now."

"And you never married?"

"No, I never did."

Don looked at her and whispered. "I'm glad you didn't. Do you suppose we could begin again?"

Jill lowered her head and then she looked up. Her eyes were sparkling. "I've been hoping to find you all my life. Now that I have, I don't want to let you go."

"Jill, even though I loved my wife, I've never gotten you out of my mind."

"What about your children—will they understand?"

"We didn't have any."

"Oh, we have so much catching up to do."

"My home is on the West coast. I could make Detroit my overnight on my runs to New York every third day. It would be a temporary situation. It will take a little time, but I could arrange things to suit us. Where are you living in Detroit?"

"I have an apartment just a short distance from here."

"That's super. Would you like to come back to the hotel or should we go to your place?"

"How about my place?"

"That's perfect and now that I have found you, I am not giving up a single moment of my time in being with you. The photography show at my hotel can go on without my personal appearance since I have all of my photo art in place."

Once inside her apartment, Don had a hard time keeping his true feelings from surfacing. He wanted to hold her and feel her warm body close to his. He wanted to smother her with kisses and never let her go. Holding hands, Jill was feeling the same way about Don. She too was struggling to hold her emotions back. As they gazed at each other, Don broke the spell.

"Jill, tell me, what happened when that plane went down?"

"We ditched in rough sea near an island. Colonel Bates miscalculated and thought it was about fifty miles from Biak. We were nearly one hundred and fifty miles from there. We found this out after we were captured by island natives."

Don could sense the tightness in her voice when she described all the events. These were difficult memories to bring back.

"The natives, did they hurt you?"

"No, they were very friendly at first. Their one junior leader, a sort of witch doctor, hated us for being white. He finally convinced the chieftain, I think, that we were unclean and should be killed. Fortunately, one of the native women had sympathy toward us. Through her, we made our escape and were taken to two islands before we were finally escorted to Biak. The escape and trip took over a month, and we weren't sure if we would get back alive. Once we were on Biak, I never saw any of the others again."

"You don't know what happened to Colonel Bates?"

"The last I heard, he was sent to Guam to command a night fighter squadron."

"Do you know anything about Jerry Hurwitz or Jordan Bond?"

"Not a word. Do you think they survived the war?"

"God, I hope so. I would love to see them again."

"Don, what happened in your life?"

"Well the accident with the P-61 grounded me in the Air Force. I couldn't stand flying a desk so I took a medical discharge. I signed on with the airlines as a copilot. After a year, I made Captain. When Betty died, I took up photography to fill up the lonely hours and to occupy my mind."

"The main thing is you stayed with what you loved the most—flying."

"Yes, only there has always been a nagging aspect to my life Jill. There are thoughts that have never left me since the crash in that jungle."

"You mean you are blaming yourself for what happened back then?"

"That's it exactly. I have never forgiven myself for that accident."

"Don, that was so long ago. Surely you don't think it matters anymore! It has probably been forgotten by everyone by now."

"Jill, I would have been court-martialed for that accident if I hadn't been sent back to the states in a body cast."

"But we all survived. You set that airplane down so skillfully. You saved our lives by struggling for miles to get help. They should have given you a medal!"

"You're very kind to say that Jill. Unfortunately the military doesn't see things that way. One officer lost his life in the rescue. I placed other lives in jeopardy—not to mention the trashing of an expensive airplane. All because I wanted to impress a girl I was mad about. I never even had the guts to tell my wife about you. I couldn't hurt her but I'm ashamed that I kept the truth from her."

Jill looked into his eyes and spoke softly. "And you've carried our secret with you all these years?"

"Yes, and now that we've found each other I want to keep you for the rest of my life."

Tears filled Jill's eyes as he pulled her toward him.

"Oh Don, if you only knew how much I've missed you—how I've longed to find you and tell you I still loved you."

Their tearful embrace rendered them both speechless. Don lifted her off the couch and carried her to the bedroom. Later, their passions spent, they lay sleeping in each other's arms till the morning sun streamed through the windowpanes.

Jill made breakfast early, knowing that Don had to fly out at ten in the morning. When he left, she counted the hours till she would hear his voice again.

Seventeen

*D*on gripped the yoke of the airliner with his left hand, and rolled in the trim tabs with his right. He set the controls on automatic pilot, sat back and turned his thoughts to the events of the last twelve hours. Finding Jill was like a dream to him. His co-pilot and flight engineer had each noticed the change in him when he boarded the plane—a certain lightness in his step.

At first they assumed it was his success with his photography show, but then they eventually suspected that something else was up. The co-pilot, Tim, finally asked, "Anything interesting happen while you were in Detroit, Captain?"

"Oh, just a miracle is all!"

"What do you mean Captain?" Tim pressed.

"I met someone out of my past—a girl I haven't seen in many years. It's a long story. We were friends in the Pacific during the war. I'd rather not go into details, only to say we fell for each other. We were separated after a short time together."

"You mean you dumped her?" Tim asked half-jokingly.

"No. She was reported lost at sea when her transport went down. I never heard from her again until last night. She phoned me at my hotel to confirm my identity after seeing my name in an advanced press release for the show. We arranged to meet."

"That's incredible! So you found out you still had feelings for her?"

"Yes, you could say that."

"Well Captain, I'm happy for you. The whole crew has been hoping you'd find someone to share your life. None of the flight attendants could figure you out. You didn't seem to have an interest in any kind of relationship after your wife died. Can I give them the good news?"

"I'd rather you didn't. I like to keep my personal life private."

"No problem Captain."

Turning his head toward the flight engineer and navigator, Don grinned and said, "That goes for you two big-eared bozos too, okay?" They both laughed and went back to their business.

Once he was back at the company's main offices, Don sought a change in his flight routes. He wanted to spend more time in Detroit, and the schedulers were happy to help him do so. The more time he spent with Jill, the more he thought of the accident that had separated them for so many years. He was forever plagued that his military career ended because of that fateful flight. Now thoughts of Jerry Hurwitz and Jordan Bond surfaced again and Don's feelings of guilt soon became a fixation. Jill noticed the change in him and quickly brought it to his attention.

"Don, I get the impression that you've been dwelling on that accident in New Guinea. What is really bothering you Honey?"

"I've held my feelings deep inside ever since it happened. It's hard to explain, but I need to somehow do something to make amends."

"Don, it's behind you. I'm sure Jerry and Jordan have forgotten it. I certainly have. But okay, if something has to happen, what do you think it will take for you to forgive yourself?"

"I haven't a clue. One thing though, I'd like to find Jerry and Tuskegee. I'd like us all to be together again."

"How will you ever find them?"

"I know Jerry was from a small town in Pennsylvania called Wilksburg. His parents were business people. Jill would you consider helping me in finding them?"

"Of course. Since I'm not too far from Pennsylvania, I could call information and see if there are any Hurwitz's in that town. I'll start early next week while you're in California. Maybe I'll have good news for you when you get back."

"Sounds great Honey. As for Jordan, I'll contact his hometown of Tuskegee, Alabama. Maybe his name will pop up in the directory. If not, I can go in another direction."

"What do you mean?"

"I've heard of the Tuskegee Airman's Association. Perhaps Jordan is a member."

The two sensed they were about to embark on a long search. Jill smiled and ran her fingers through Don's hair. If finding them would help to erase some of Don's painful memories, then she was more than willing to help him. As soon as Don flew out, Jill enthusiastically began her mission. She dialed information for Wilksburg, Pennsylvania for a listing under the name Jerry Hurwitz. She found none. Undaunted, she asked if there were any other Hurwitz's listed. Given the number of an Addam Hurwitz, she called the number hoping he was related to Jerry.

"I wish I could help you mam, but the Jerry whose family owned the local furniture store moved to California several years ago. We were distant cousins. I've lost track of him over the years."

"Do you know what part of California he relocated to?"

"I'm not sure about that but my guess is somewhere near the San Francisco Bay area. That's all I can tell you."

"Well, it's a start. Thank you so much for the information. I guess there are no other relatives or friends I could contact in your area?"

"No, I'm afraid they are all gone."

"Thanks anyway Mr. Hurwitz."

Jill considered the best approach for finding Jerry would be to search in the bay area but she decided to leave it up to Don.

Meanwhile, Don eagerly began his search by calling Tuskegee, Alabama information. Jordan was not listed. Then he called the Air Force Association Magazine in Washington, D.C., seeking information about the Tuskegee Airmen's Association. They obligingly gave him a contact number. Don was very surprised and disappointed to learn that Jordan's name was not on the membership roster. Failing that approach, another idea struck him. He called the Air Force Headquarters in Washington, D.C. They indicated that all records regarding WWII Veterans were kept in St. Louis. When he called St. Louis they told him that a fire had destroyed all the files alphabetically from A through S. He was back to square one.

Jill met Don at the airport in Detroit. At dinner, their conversation quickly turned to their progress in their search.

"What did you find out about Jerry?" Don began.

"Believe it or not, Jerry's cousin thought that Jerry had moved to the Bay Area in California years ago. But he didn't know exactly where."

"Well, at least you have some clues. I hit a dead end. There are no records available on Jordan—not in Tuskegee or from the Air Force files, which were destroyed in a fire. I'll concentrate on the Bay Area when I get back."

Jill suggested they place an ad in the Air Force Magazine to read: Friends desire to contact Jordan Bond—Air Force flying officer with the Air Transport Command and former P-51 fighter pilot with the Tuskegee Airmen. Also served in the South Pacific. Please contact Jill Harris or Don Jennings at P.O. Box P-61, Detroit, MI 48066 or call (313) 766-7913.

Satisfied with the wording, they both agreed to write up a similar ad for Jerry Hurwitz. Excitedly, they dashed to the closest corner mailbox and deposited their letters.

Eighteen

Jerry Hurwitz sat on his veranda, on Balboa Island in southern California, overlooking the blue Pacific. His wife Lillian had just poured him another cup of coffee and handed him the mail. Lillian was happy caring for her distinguished-looking man, with his shock of wavy white hair and air of calmness about him. As he sorted his mail, Jerry glanced through his copy of the Air Force Magazine. The magazine was a gift subscription from a friend and Jerry probably wouldn't have initially subscribed to it himself. His eyes fell upon a large bold face ad. He shook his head in disbelief. "Lillian, you won't believe what I just read!"

"What is it darling?"

"An old Air Force buddy is trying to contact me. Don Jennings was the pilot I trained and served with in the South Pacific."

"Where is he now?"

"Apparently in Detroit, Michigan. At least that's the address in the ad."

"Let me see it, dear. Who is Jill Harris?"

"Oh, she was a friend of ours—an Air Force WAAC."

"You mean a girlfriend of this man Don Jennings?"

"Well, I think she was more of a friend than a girlfriend. Evidently they have kept in touch through the years. Now they are looking for me and Jordan Bond."

"Who is Jordan Bond?"

"He was a black Air Force transport pilot we met in New Guinea."

"I guess you were pretty close at one time for them to want to find you after all these years."

Jerry shrugged his shoulders. She sensed that he didn't want to discuss it.

"Why do you suppose they are looking for you?" Lillian pressed.

"I really don't know. I guess they must be working up a reunion of Air Force buddies. I'm not really interested." He tossed the magazine aside and picked up the newspaper.

Lillian was surprised at Jerry's reaction. She brushed the newspaper away from his face. Jerry's eyes were very moist.

"Honey, there's something you don't want to talk about, isn't there?"

"Please leave it alone sweetie. I don't like to talk about those days in the service."

He had never discussed his military life with her. Lillian decided to drop the subject, and went back to clearing the coffee cups from the table. But her interest had been aroused, and when the time was right, she would respond to that ad herself.

Jerry had married Lillian a few weeks after the war ended. Their courtship was brief, but they were very much in love. And though they were from different social backgrounds, they communicated almost as if they were of one mind. Jerry was a sales representative for a large sports company. He traveled worldwide until his retirement at age fifty. He devoted his spare time to golfing and yard work. Lillian came from an Irish heritage. She was active in volunteer work since her retirement, and she served as an editor for a small weekly newspaper. Jerry and Lillian were members of the local country club where they played bridge and golf. Their religious and social backgrounds had never interfered with how they felt about each other, and now they had been together, happily, for twenty years.

The mystery of Jerry's past had always bothered Lillian. Now that others were making inquiries, she was determined to find out about Jerry's military life. The next morning, as soon as Jerry left to play a round of golf with his friend, Lillian hurried to the phone and dialed the number listed in the ad. Jill had just stepped out of the shower when the phone rang, and the operator asked if she would accept a collect call from Lillian Hurwitz in California.

"Oh yes, I will!" Jill said excitedly.

"Good morning, Miss Harris. I'm calling about your ad in the Air Force Magazine regarding my husband Jerry. I couldn't get him to respond so I'm taking the liberty to find out what this is about."

"Oh I see. Well to give you some background, Don Jennings and I are companions. We both knew Jerry in the South Pacific. In fact Don, Jerry, Jordan and I shared a harrowing experience."

Lillian was on the edge of her chair. "What happened?"

"We survived a horrible crash in the jungles of New Guinea back in 1945."

"Oh my. And you haven't seen each other for how long?"

"Well over twenty years!"

"You would have so much to talk about if you got together. I must tell you though, Jerry doesn't seem to be interested in responding to your ad. In fact, he never told me anything about his war experiences."

"I can't imagine that Mrs. Hurwitz."

"Oh, please call me Lillian."

"That's so nice of you and please call me Jill. I just can't understand why Jerry wouldn't want to see us again. We are certainly anxious to see him."

"I can only suggest that you give Jerry a call when he returns from his golf game. He should be home around eleven o'clock."

"Lillian, Don will be so excited when he hears we've found Jerry."

"Isn't Mr. Jennings there with you?"

"No, as a matter of fact he's in California too! He's an airline Captain flying out of Los Angeles. Don lives in the valley but stays here in Detroit about four days a week. I will have him call Jerry as soon as he arrives here later today."

"Please don't let Mr. Jennings tell Jerry how he found his phone number. I think Jerry would be upset with me if he knew I was the one who tipped you off."

"You have my word on it. Don can say he found Jerry's name while leafing through the phone book."

"Good thinking. I'll be anxious to see how Jerry reacts when Mr. Jennings calls. I hope you have luck in finding Jordan Bond too. Perhaps Jerry might know where he is."

"Thank you for being so helpful. I'm looking forward to meeting you. Good-bye for now and we'll be talking again soon."

When Don arrived back in Detroit, Jill told him about Lillian's phone call. Don was excited but puzzled over Jerry's attitude. He immediately called, and by Don's tone of voice, Jill could tell Jerry was receptive. After the conversation, Don was elated!

"He's fine. He will meet with me as soon as I get back to L.A."

"That's wonderful. Does he know where to find Jordan?"

"He said he didn't, but he had some ideas. He'll try to find some information before we meet."

"Lillian, how do you suppose Don Jennings got my phone number?"

"Didn't he tell you?" Lillian stalled.

"I assumed you had called and gave it to him."

Unable to lie to Jerry, Lillian confessed. Jerry smiled and said, "I'm glad you did."

Jerry was relieved and ready to see his old friends again. "Lillian, I have carried this burden around too long. Don and I were close buddies. We had trained together. I was his radar operator with the P-61 night fighters. I was even his best man at his wedding before we left for the South Pacific. We ate, slept, and flew together daily for over a year before being sent to tackle the Japanese Air Force. We thought we would win the war by knocking them down at night. Unfortunately for us, things didn't work out that way. We arrived on the islands in October 1944. We waited until December for P-61's to arrive from the States. When one finally arrived, it was assigned to us We were waiting for orders to fly our first combat mission. The CO made the decision to wait until we obtained a few more airplanes before sending us out on combat duty. Meanwhile, Don was anxious to get going. We went to the Officer's Club one night, and met this transport pilot, 'Tuskegee' Bond. We both took a liking to him. Bond was a decorated P-51 fighter ace in the Italian campaign. Later he retrained as a transport command pilot and flew supplies and troops to the South Pacific. He was interested in flying on a P-61 night fighter so Don asked if he would like to go along the next time we went up."

Lillian interrupted, "What about Jill Harris? Where did she come into the picture?"

"Jill was in intelligence; a non-commissioned officer. Don met her in the operation's office. They became friends. Why, I don't know, but Don invited Jill to come along on the flight too. To demonstrate the power of the P-61, Don climbed out steeply to clear a 5,000-foot mountain, five miles from the end of the runway. He couldn't get the altitude on his first try so he pealed away, then headed back to try again. It looked like we were going to make it this time. But at the top of the climb, the aircraft started to fall off on the left wing. I knew we were in real trouble. We were too close to the peak. Suddenly we were falling tail first. We pancaked right into the trees!"

"My God Jerry, did you get hurt?"

"I had a bad gash on my head when I was thrown out of the plane on impact. Jill had an ankle sprain. Don and Jordan were bruised but okay."

Jerry related the incidents following the crash, first recounting Don's fall over the waterfalls and broken back, and their cold nights on the mountain while awaiting rescue. Jerry told her in detail about their trek down the mountain and attack

177

by the Japanese sniper. He described his strong attachment to the three comrades, and their eventual separation. Then Jerry expressed his chagrin— mainly of subsequent events, of being maligned as a "Jew Boy" who had been partly responsible for trashing the airplane. While he was never angry with Don for what had happened, he had been left behind to face the music and the anti-Semitic treatment he experienced afterward. When he finished his story, he paused, looked into Lillian's eyes and simply said, "I'm glad that's off my chest."

Lillian was in tears when he ended his story. "I'm so glad you have found your friends. It will do you good to see them again. When are you meeting Don?"

"Day after tomorrow."

"I'm anxious to meet him too. But since you two have so much catching up to do I will leave you to yourselves."

"That's so thoughtful of you hon. I'm sure you will like him. He's a hell of a guy!"

Don made his way through a maze of traffic, south out of L.A. He headed toward Newport Beach, where he caught the ferry to Balboa Island. He was impressed with the flower-lined streets and the magnificent beach houses along the way. Every cottage was adorned with floral displays and quaint, small gardens at their entrances. Jerry's house was nestled behind a white picket fence on a corner lot facing the beach. A bright blue Cadillac in the driveway boasted a license tag, RETIRED-2.

He rang the bell and in seconds the unmistakable figure of his old buddy was standing in the doorway.

"You look great!" Don said as he shook his friend's hand.

"Man, you haven't changed a bit!"

"Well I wish that were true old buddy. The years have a way of telling on all of us. We have to keep our sense of humor, 'cause getting older ain't for sissies!"

Jerry laughed heartily.

Lillian could see instantly that a strong bond still existed between the two men. Shortly after Jerry introduced her, Lillian said, "I know you two have a great deal to talk about, so I'll leave you alone for awhile and I'll do some shopping. I will be home in plenty of time to fix dinner. How does that sound?"

"Fine honey."

Lillian bid them farewell and headed out the door.

"Well my friend, how about a walk on the beach? I'll show you where I spend a lot of my time."

They walked the beach for two hours. Don listened earnestly to Jerry's account of what had transpired during his remaining time in the service. He felt badly when Jerry told him how he had been treated because he was Jewish.

Soon the discussion turned to Betty and the wonderful life they had together before her passing. Jerry was saddened to learn that Betty died so young. Then Don changed the subject and related that he was at a dead end in finding Jordan.

"I can't imagine why he wouldn't be listed among the Tuskegee Airmen right there in Tuskegee, Alabama. Do you think he is still alive?" Jerry asked.

"I'm betting he is. He's a survivor. We just have to keep on trying."

"Do you think he would be an active member of the NAACP? He openly detested his treatment in the service because of his color," Jerry added.

"Let's make a call to the NAACP in Tuskegee, when we get back to your house, okay?"

The two men quickened their pace as they headed back. Lillian was getting out of the car, and the two men helped her unload a trunk full of groceries.

"You two just relax in the den and I'll prepare dinner," she insisted.

Jerry dialed long distance information, and within minutes he had the NAACP. Jerry was smiling broadly when he hung up the phone. He wrote some information on a notepad.

"Buddy, we've struck pay dirt! Tuskegee is a member. He lives in Goshen, Alabama; here's his phone number. I'd like you to call him."

Don insisted that Jerry talk to him first, and Jerry dialed the number. "Now I hope you don't think this is a crank call. Do you remember your old friend from the P-61 crash in New Guinea, Jerry Hurwitz?"

"Are you putting me on Sir?"

"No indeed, is this Jordan 'Tuskegee' Bond?"

"Jerry, is it really you? How the hell are you?"

"I'm looking well," Jerry jokingly replied. "Listen, I have another surprise for you. Someone here wants to say hello to you."

"Jordan? It's me, Don Jennings. How are you old friend?"

"I just can't believe all this. What are you guys up to?"

"To tell you the truth, I just met with Jerry today. I also have to tell you that Jill Harris and I are companions as well!"

"Are you serious? I thought she was dead!"

"I thought so too until a few weeks ago. She contacted me in Detroit. We've been together ever since."

"I can hardly believe my ears!"

"We'd like to get together with you. What does your calendar look like?"

"Don, I don't have a calendar anymore. I tossed that thing out two years ago when I retired from the Space Administration in Huntsville. I'm free to travel anytime. Of course my wife travels with me wherever I go. Where would you like to meet?"

"Jerry, where and when would it be convenient for you and Lillian to meet?"

"Since Jill is in Detroit and we're here, perhaps Jordan could wing it to Chicago next week."

Don relayed this suggestion to Jordan. He was agreeable, and they settled on a Saturday meeting at the Harbor House Hotel on the lake.

Lillian called the men to dinner. She had prepared a delicious meal and the three chattered on about the upcoming reunion. That evening Don called Jill and when Jill learned of the reunion, she was thrilled. Later that week she made her plans to go to Chicago, and Don made reservations at the hotel for a suite of rooms and routed himself to lay over in Chicago for three days on his next run to New York.

Nineteen

A gorgeous woman turned several male heads as she stepped out of the taxi in front of the Harbor House Hotel. Jill Harris quickly placed her handbag in front of her to prevent her skirt from flying up in the wild Chicago wind, and the doorman escorted her into the hotel lobby. At the front desk she was told that Don Jennings had not yet checked in, so she decided to sit in the lobby to wait for him. She was a little early, but she knew he would be on time—he was always punctual.

Jill tried to imagine what Jordan and Jerry would look like. She pictured Jerry as having grown stocky. Jordan would show signs of graying, but she couldn't imagine him with any wrinkles or lines on his face. She wondered if she would be able to recognize them in a crowd.

Ten minutes elapsed and Don came through the door wearing his airline uniform. They embraced, and he kissed her lovingly.

"Any signs of our guests?"

"Not yet."

"Well, it's early. I'm sure they'll be here soon. Why don't we go up to the suite, and I'll change into street clothes," Don suggested.

The large and luxurious suite was decorated in mauve colors and fresh roses adorned the spacious living room.

"Oh Don. This place is out of this world!"

"I'm glad you like it Jill. I wanted the best suite they had for this occasion."

Within minutes, Jerry and Lillian arrived. Jill gave Jerry a big hug and kissed him on the cheek. Memories of their past flashed through their minds as they stood tearfully looking at one another.

"Jerry, you look just like I imagined you would!"

"Jill, you look magnificent!" Turning to Lillian he said, "This is my long lost friend."

"Jill, I'm so glad to finally meet you!"

"Thank you. You were so sweet to get back to me and help me pull these guys together after all these years."

As the foursome chatted away, another knock on the door silenced them. Don opened the door to find a distinguished-looking couple, one of whom was grinning from ear to ear. Don grabbed Jordan's hand to shake it as Jordan leaned in and gave Don a manly hug. Don turned to usher them into the living room just as Jill arrived on the run to hug Jordan. Jerry was right behind her and started patting Jordan's back as Jill finished the hug. Eventually Jordan stepped back and introduced his wife Marsha. They all greeted each other warmly, making Lillian and Marsha know that they were part of the inner circle of this foursome's reunion. When the greetings finally ended, Don asked Jordan how things had gone for him after he had delivered Don to the base hospital at Marsh Field. Jordan said that he had spent the rest of the war flying troops and cargo all over the South Pacific. He made a career out of the service and attained the rank of Lieutenant Colonel before his retirement.

"What about the crap you had to put up with during the war?" Jerry queried.

"I've tried to forget that period of my life. After the war it wasn't so bad in the north. When I was stationed in the south, once I left the base it was a whole different story; not much different than when I was growing up and we would have to go into a white town. You know segregation didn't exactly end when President Eisenhower forced integration of the schools in Mississippi. Things really didn't get too much better until the Kennedy and Johnson administration and then the actual forced integration was gut wrenching. Of course we all know that voluntary segregation became the way of life, essentially everywhere, with whites moving out of any area or community that blacks chose to move into. Integration has actually hurt our schools and our black kids have lost the educational incentives they once had in the segregated Deep South. Okay, I'll get off of the soapbox. I finally have felt some respect in the last 10 years, but integration has been a long struggle for our people. Now we are working on the trickier and subtler long-term problem of achieving equality."

"Well buddy we have a little something in common on that score. Us Jew boys have had our taste of prejudice ever since I can remember," Jerry added.

"Both of you guys have weathered the social injustices thrown your way," Don remarked sympathetically.

"Jill, we're anxious to hear about your past," Lillian piped in, changing the subject.

Charming and eloquent as she spoke, Jill credited Don's skillful forced landing with the P-61 and his treacherous journey down the mountain with saving their lives. Then the group listened intently as Jill told them about her escape from the jungles of New Guinea after the crash at sea.

When the hour grew late, the group retired to their respective rooms. And then as Don lay beside Jill, he thought about what was left unsaid.

Jill whispered softly into his ear, "How do you feel about things now?"

"It's been a wonderful day. I hated to see it end."

"We all talked about our lives except you dear. It'll be your turn tomorrow. Are you going to tell them how you've really felt all these years?"

"I am not sure how I will approach the subject sweetie. I hope something comes up that will help me overcome this awful guilt complex."

"Don, can't you tell those two men hold no ill-feelings toward you? Why can't you accept their love and understanding?"

"I just can't help thinking about what happened to Jerry. His life was miserable after the crash. I escaped all the ridicule. And you were damned near killed again because of what I did! Maybe Jordan would have been treated more respectfully if he had not been associated with my accident."

"Don, I don't think that accident had a bearing on how Jordan was treated. Black men were discriminated against in all branches of the service during the war. Jordan knows you respected him highly."

Don didn't respond. She added, "Let's not think about it anymore tonight. We need to get some sleep." He could tell Jill was tired, so he kissed her goodnight. She snuggled up close—fully secure at his side.

The next morning Don rose before anyone else. He dialed room service and ordered breakfast. Jerry and Jordan both emerged from their bedrooms at the same time. Don laughed to see the three of them up before the ladies. He joked that they were up and moving by the crack of dawn—the Army

187

way. Just as Don was finishing his remark, Jill entered the room.

"You haven't lost the habit either," Don said happily.

When breakfast arrived, Marsha and Lillian joined them. They all spoke casually throughout the meal. Finally Jordan turned to Don and asked, "What happened after I bid you goodbye at the Marsh Air Force base hospital?"

Don told them about his recovery from his broken back. He talked about his feelings for Jill and how saddened he was to hear of her death. Being mindful and sensitive to Jill's feelings, he related his life with Betty and her tragic struggle with breast cancer. He expressed his loneliness after her death and how his airline career and his photography hobby filled the void. He told them how Jill came back into his life. Finally he disclosed his torment from the P-61 crash and how he harbored great guilt over causing them all such heartache.

Jerry quickly spoke up, "Don, I never blamed you for what happened to me in the military. My experience with you as my pilot was the greatest part of my military career."

Jordan instantly agreed with Jerry.

Jill added, "You can't change what happened to that aircraft. Thousands were lost to accidents and enemy fire during that war."

"But guys, don't you get it? I destroyed the only combat airplane our squadron had received! Lt. Keaton was killed by a sniper during your trek down the mountain. Apparently my actions caused you to be orphaned as a radar operator Jerry! Jill, you were transferred out of your squadron away from your friends. Look how I placed you in danger, Jordan after what you had faced in Europe. And then I caused Commander Bates a lot of grief because of that accident! No...I can't forget what a mess I made of everything just because I wanted to give you guys a thrill! I have carried these feelings for a long time. I have to find a way to make things right. Do any of you have any ideas?"

The room was silent after Don's confession. Finally Jerry spoke with deep sincerity.

"Don, maybe you're making more out of this than you need to. If we could find out how the other squadron members felt about that incident, then maybe we could dispel some of your anxiety. I know of the World War II Night Fighters Association based in California. Maybe we could get some feedback from some of the veterans who were over there with us."

"You mean you want me to air my feelings to them?"

"Not exactly Don. I mean we could get a feel for their thinking by just associating ourselves with them. We could attend one of their meetings."

"It might be a long shot, but that may not be a bad idea; and I'm willing to try it. If you find out when they meet Jerry then I will arrange to be there with you."

Lillian wondered how Jerry would face his WWII peers after what had happened to him in the service. She silently hoped he wasn't "opening a can of worms."

Jordan agreed that since they were both Night Fighters they should attend.

After these decisions were made, the group decided to catch a show after dinner. Happy and exhausted, they returned to their hotel at 2:00 a.m.

They put in a final light-hearted day of touring the sights of Chicago and then said their goodbyes. Jill had that warm feeling that something wonderful had taken place, and Don felt it too. With a voice of confidence, he remarked, "Honey, I think we are about to embark on a very interesting journey. My instincts tell me this trip with Jerry is the right way to go."

Jill did not confide her feelings but thought to herself, "Don is having remorse over an incident that had tarnished his pride. These three men were exceptional and responsible individuals; together they were an unusually diverse threesome that just clicked. They were proud men, and rightly so, who had always done the best they could, and they were so very proud of their accomplishments. It is apparent to me that these three wore more than their WWII silver wings—they wore wings of pride as well."

Twenty

*D*on received a call from Jerry, saying that he had made reservations for them to go to the Night Fighters Annual Convention in Long Beach. Jerry had checked just in time as the convention was starting that next weekend.

When they checked into their room and sat down to review the program, they were shocked to see the name Joseph Bates, retired Brigadier General, listed on the guest register! Both respected Bates greatly and were anxious to see him again. And on the next page of the list, Lou Flarety's name jumped out.

"Lou was damn near killed on the way back down, when the sniper opened up on us. We became pretty good friends after you left, Don. It will be good to see him again. Looks like Bates and Fraley are the only two names we know, but that is more than good enough."

Don and Jerry wanted to be anonymous, so they thought it wise to use fictitious names when they registered. Jerry used the name Dale Hill and Don was Jack Carson.

When the two men sat down at one of the round tables, most of the other men were accompanied by their spouses. Don and Jerry explained that they were widowed.

All the other men at their table were members of the 51st Squadron in the South Pacific Theater. Don and Jerry were also members of this squadron, but they didn't recognize any of the others, and none of the other men recognized them.

Jerry wasted no time and joked about a story he had heard—a non-combat incident in New Guinea involving a P-61 and four crewmembers. A short, stocky man recalled the incident instantly. He said that some "smart-ass hot-shot" pilot had trashed the only P-61 they had received from the States. He recalled that the three-man aircraft had four crew aboard when it went in, and one of the crew was a WACC! Another man with a well- trimmed beard recalled the crash too. He remembered that the rescue team was attacked and his good friend, Lt. Keaton was killed.

"Too bad the pilot got away with it. They sent him back to the States in a hurry," he said sarcastically.

Jerry asked if they ever found out why the WACC was on board.

The stocky man said, "I know she was assigned to the operations office. Why she was on board, no one ever seemed to know. They hushed the whole damn thing up as fast as they could. Seems like the OR on board hung around for a long time, but he never got much flight time after his pilot was sent back to the States."

"All I know is that Lt. Keaton was buried on the field and the girl and the two other crewmen just faded away," added the other man.

"Does anyone know what caused the crash?" Don questioned.

"Hell, they never found out. The plane crashed into such a remote jungle it couldn't be salvaged. As far as I know, the damn airplane is still sitting up on that mountain. Too bad, too. They say it was hardly damaged," said the stocky man.

A third man joined in. "As far as I am concerned, we lost more than Lt. Keaton and an airplane. Things were messed up for a good while, and a bunch of people wasted a lot of time, and precious resources, and then we almost lost our squadron commander, Joe Bates. After that crash, Joe went down on his way to Biak to pick up another P-61 to replace the one we lost. He was a damn good commander."

"Oh I remember that now. He was flying a gooney bird, the old C-47, when he went down."

"I heard that not only did Bates go down, but the WACC who was aboard the downed P-61 was on that flight with Bates. We can never get Bates to talk about that flight," the stocky man said as he pointed to a table at the far end of the room where Bates was sitting.

"I would be interested in learning more details and the whole truth about that incident. I'd like to write, and maybe I would do a story on it."

"If you want to know more on it, you could catch Lou Flarety or Joe Bates while you're here. They could give you the full scoop—if they are willing to talk about it. But good luck."

Feigning ignorance, Don said, "You mean Lou Flarety is also here?"

"Oh yeah, I saw him," one of the men said.

Turning to Don, Jerry remarked, "That's a good idea. I'll track them down while we're here, Jack."

The following day they sat in on many of the meetings. The organization's main theme was to promote awareness of the role the Night Fighters had played in the European and Pacific Theaters during WWII. In addition, they were trying to get squadrons to hold state meetings and increase their memberships and activities. During one of the general meetings, Don and Jerry encountered Joseph Bates. Handsome and distinguished, his graying hair was still wavy and well groomed. He walked smartly into the room to conduct the afternoon meeting.

"Jesus," Don whispered. "He hasn't changed much!"

"The years have treated him well. It will be interesting to hear what he has to say," Jerry responded.

Joe Bates encouraged the group to take part in the discussions and to offer any suggestions for the good of the order. Discussions seem to center on the role of the P-61. The pilots from the British Beaufighter Night Fighters in the European theater expressed concern that their role was being overshadowed. Bates smiled because he had played a major role by flying the Beaufighter in combat in Europe before the P-61 was introduced. He told them that most of the Beaufighter pilots had made the transition into the P-61 before the war ended in Europe, and that the P-61 distinguished itself in the Pacific war far more than it did in Europe. He made the point that any Night Fighter who flew the Beaufighter should not be offended. They would always be recognized as an important part of the association—they were not a separate entity. They were all to be known as "Night Fighters."

At one point a member posed an interesting question. He asked Bates if he knew of any P-61's still flying in the world.

"I don't know of any flying today. As a matter of fact, I am aware of only three planes that exist. They are all standing in museums on static display. That's not very many considering there were over seven hundred made during the war."

One of the members in the middle of the room raised his hand to be recognized.

"Yes Sir, what is your question?"

"Sir, I believe there are four P-61's remaining."

"Do you know the location of the fourth one?"

"I have it on good authority that there is one still resting on a mountain top in New Guinea." Bates' face reddened a little. He urged the man to continue.

"This airplane crashed there in 1945. It was on a routine mission and had just taken off from the field. The pilot tried to climb over the mountain but stalled out and went into the jungle about 5,000 feet up and just 200 feet short of clearing the mountain peak."

"Yes, I am aware of that crash. But how do you know the plane is still there after all these years?"

"I know because the missionary from our church saw it when he was serving in the area last year," the man confirmed.

"Did the missionary describe the condition of the plane?"

"Yes. He maintained that the jungle foliage had protected the aircraft; there was hardly any damage to it. He said there is even air in the tires."

Bates commented, "Knowing that country, I'm sure there is no way that aircraft could be taken off that rough mountain. There would be no ground access by road or even a path."

Don's heart was pounding by this time and his mind was racing.

"Jerry," Don whispered. "We have to talk to that man who just spoke about our airplane. Don't let him out of your sight; we'll corner him as soon as the meeting is over."

Jerry looked baffled. He hadn't the slightest idea of what Don was up to. Unable to sit through the rest of the meeting, Don quietly slipped to the back of the room and lit a cigarette, and waited.

When the meeting ended, Jerry found the man Don wanted to talk to; Don was already talking with him. Don wrote down the address of the missionary and thanked the man. Just as he and Jerry were about to leave, Joe Bates walked up to them.

"Correct me if I'm wrong but you two are Don Jennings and Jerry Hurwitz."

"Your memory is excellent. It's so good to see you again after all these years General Bates. I never thought I'd see you again," Don responded enthusiastically.

"Jerry, you're looking really good. How's the world treating you?"

"Just great General," Jerry said with a broad smile.

"I'm really glad to see both of you here. I hadn't noticed your names on the attendance list. I've been a member of this association for the past seven years. By the way, we don't need to stand on rank here. I'm just Joe Bates to everyone. Say, why don't we have lunch together? I'm free for the rest of the afternoon. We could go to a little café just down the street where they have excellent food."

At the café, the three men ordered up, and then Joe Bates opened the conversation by expressing his concern over Don's injury that cut his combat pilot career short. In addition, Joe indicated his respect for Jill Harris—he understood why a person of her curiosity would be anxious to ride in a fighter plane. Joe informed them that Jill was a brave girl and had, in a sense, saved his life.

Don felt compelled to reveal that Jill was now a part of his life. He explained how they were brought together again and added that he and Jill were engaged. Astonished, Joe extended his hand and offered his congratulations.

Continuing the conversation, Bates recounted what he knew of Jerry's remaining service days. He was aware of the cruelty to Jerry due to the accident and his religion. Bates confessed he felt shame and disgust for what Jerry endured. He had learned about Jerry from some squadron officers who were transferred to Leyte Island where he was stationed at one point.

"Don, I have to say I was disappointed about the incident but I'm glad you had to be sent back to the States. Headquarters would have opted for your scalp once they received the report. They would have pushed for a court-martial. Fortunately, neither of us was around by the time the report reached them."

"You know Joe, I have never forgiven myself for that accident. It's the real reason I have come to this convention today—to find out if the Night Fighters had forgotten about the incident. It didn't take long to find out the answer. To sum up the consensus, one man said, "Some smart-ass hot-pilot trashed our only P-61." I wish he would have said the engine quit and the pilot was forced to crash land in the jungle."

"I'm not so sure Don is reaching the right conclusion," Jerry said. "I know that I never blamed Don for that accident. He proved the P-61 wasn't as good as everyone thought on its rate of climb. Also he put that plane down better than many pilots could have done and Don risked his life to save ours."

Bates listened tentatively. He never forgot that Don and Jerry had saved his own life. He was more convinced of their true characters when he heard why they came to the convention.

As the three dined, Bates posed another question. "What must take place to change your mind about that incident? The accident literally cost you your military flying career. Wasn't that punishment enough for one mistake? And what about you Jerry? How do you feel now about what happened to you back then?"

"I couldn't undo the past. I simply put it behind me and never spoke of it after the war ended. I basically came to this meeting to help Don put his past behind him."

"Well Don?" Bates asked.

"One thing today has struck me like a bolt of lightning. When I heard the wreckage was in a restorative state, I realized what I want to do. I need to get the airplane back and restore it to flight. If the association members and the rest of the world can see it fly again, then I believe I could feel vindicated."

"You don't really think you can pull that off, do you?"

"I'd like to try. First of all I have to know more than I know now. I'll have to talk to that missionary who has seen the airplane."

"Don, a project like that would cost a fortune. Also, that plane is in another country. It won't be easy to get them to release it to you. They'll ask a hefty price," Bates emphasized.

"Those things will be resolved, one by one. Other peoples have retrieved vintage airplanes out of foreign countries since the war. A lot of work will be involved, but imagine the satisfaction. We would have the only flying P-61 in the world!"

"Excuse me for putting a damper on things too, but where are you going to get the money to finance such a project?" Jerry prodded.

"If there's a will, there's a way. First I have to find out if it's recoverable."

"Perhaps we could go into a joint venture. Many big projects are done that way for funding purposes," Bates suggested.

"Do you guys want to get into this kind of venture with me?" Don asked.

"It sounds interesting as hell. What about you Jerry?" Bates commented.

"If Don finds out it can be done, then yes, I'd put whatever I can into the project. Since Don is still an active pilot and I assume he'll fly it, I'd want the privilege of sitting in the radar control seat on the first flight!" Jerry exclaimed.

"Okay Don. You find out what you can and let me know your plans. Here's my address and phone number. Let's not discuss this plan with anyone except our wives," Bates stressed.

As he made his way back to the valley, Don stopped off at a 7-Eleven and called Jill. He told her he needed to make a trip to Ohio as soon as he got back to Detroit. She did not question him but only promised to be ready when he arrived.

Upon his arrival in Detroit, Don immediately called the missionary in Ohio. Luckily the minister was home and agreed to see him. The trip was less than one hundred miles—just outside Toledo. Don could hardly contain his excitement. Tomorrow would either be a beginning or an end to his plan for vindication.

Twenty-One

*D*on exited the cockpit and headed up the tubes to the terminal, where Jill was waiting when he stepped onto the concourse. He hugged her tightly, oblivious to those around them. Her curiosity finally got the best of her and she blurted out, "All right, tell me sweetie, what's this trip all about?"

"Honey you're going to think I lost my mind when I tell you what has happened."

"Oh please tell me we're off to get married and we're going to honeymoon in Toledo," she joked.

"That isn't quite it. The truth is, dear, we're off to see the wizard...so to speak. Jerry and I made an incredible discovery at our meeting with the Night Fighter's Association."

As Don revealed the whole story in detail, Jill hung on every word. She was surprised to learn that Joe Bates was at the meeting; she hadn't thought of Joe for years. When Don told her of the likely good condition of the plane and of the possibility of recovering the plane for restoration, she was overwhelmed.

"Don, that's incredible! But if the plane really is in good shape, how will you get it off the mountain and back here? And what about the cost?"

"Whoa—slow down. I haven't had time to figure out all the details. I'll deal with each one of those aspects as we go along. What I need to know is, do you think it's worth a try? To me it seems the only way to get this monkey off my back."

"Of course it's worth a try. And I do understand, Sweetheart. Let's not dwell on it until we see the man in Toledo though."

Don heaved a sigh of relief. He looked into her face and saw that special gleam in her eye. That shining light always appeared brighter when she was excited about something.

The next day, as they headed down the Dixie highway toward Ohio, Don upped the cruise speed on his late model rental. The Reverend James Hargis was Pastor of Christ Church in the suburbs, and the parsonage was next door to the church. After two rings of the doorbell, the door opened and a short man in his late forties stood before them.

Don and Jill introduced themselves. "Thank you for seeing us," Don began.

"Please sit down folks and I'll get you something to drink."

After returning with the drinks, the minister asked, "What do you want to talk about? And if I may indulge myself before you answer, let me add that, yes, I do perform weddings for folks outside our church membership. And, no, I'm not a mind reader; it's just obvious that you two are in love and very excited about something. Well, did I get it right?"

"Pastor, you sure have described us to a tee. But there is another reason that we've come here today. I've been told that while you were a missionary in Irian Jaya, you saw the wreckage of an old WWII military plane atop a mountain."

"Yes, I served as a missionary near an old American airfield just at the foot of the mountain in the eastern part."

"We are familiar with the Capur Air Base you speak of. Both of us served there during the war."

"I see. Well, I taught the natives from the surrounding villages during my tenure of three years. I was told by some of the natives about an American aircraft that lay high up on the mountain. I had to see it for myself. It was a difficult journey but well worth the effort. The old warplane was sitting there in a ghostly fashion, with the jungle foliage nearly covering it. I was astounded by it's well-preserved condition. I looked into the wheel wells, and I could see the tires were still inflated!"

"Has anyone else ever contacted you about this plane?"

"Yes, I received a call several months ago from a man in Florida. I was reluctant to give him any information over the phone. He was apparently upset about this and hung up on me. He never even told me his name."

"Reverend, I need to tell you something. I was the pilot of that aircraft you saw. Jill was also aboard when we went in."

"Really! It must have been quite an experience for both of you. I never heard anything about the crew. I'm happy to see that you are both alive and well."

"Well, I'm going to ask you to keep our conversation in confidence and our meeting here today a secret. My reason is that we are going to try to bring the airplane down from that mountain. I just wouldn't want anyone to know about these plans, yet."

"You have my word on it, Mr. Jennings."

With grateful handshakes, Don and Jill thanked him and said their goodbyes. As soon as they were in the car, Don hugged Jill tightly. "Honey, do you know what I'm thinking?"

Jill smiled and slyly said, "Let me guess...you have made up your mind to embark on a quest?"

"I need to do a lot of research and preparation work to even attempt to recover that baby. If you will help me, I think we can convince the others to assist too."

Jill knew this project would be long and difficult. All she really wanted was for Don to marry her and take her back to his home in California. "Don, you know I love you and I want you to be totally happy. This may sound selfish, but I wish we could be together while we work on this project—not two thousand miles away from each other."

Don realized that he should have asked her to marry him. He felt ashamed that he hadn't.

"Sweetheart, I want that too. Will you marry me?"

Jill was embarrassed. She had no intention of pressuring him into a proposal. "Oh Don, I didn't mean to suggest you quit flying just to be with me."

"Nonsense, I'm not going to quit flying. I just want to quit the Airlines. I'm eligible to retire, with full benefits. I'll have plenty of time to devote to this project. Will you marry me and leave your job too?" Don pleaded.

"I will! I'll resign right away and fly home with you."

Don put his arms around her and drew her close. "You've made me very happy. I never thought you wanted to give up your career and move to California. I guess that is why I never asked you to marry me."

As they drove on, Jill said that she did not want a formal wedding and they agreed to be married by a Justice of the Peace.

The following day Don made his way to the kitchen, brewed some coffee, sat down and outlined a tentative plan of action for the project.

Jill wound up her affairs at her office, notified her landlord she was moving, and was ready to leave with Don on his flight to L.A.

With Don up front in the cockpit, Jill sat contentedly in the first class section—close enough to feel his presence. The next day they were married in a tiny town near Van Nuys, and Don retired from the Airlines. And they immediately began working on Don's outlined plan for the project.

Shortly they had commitments from Jerry, Jordan and Joe Bates for their first expedition to the crash site. They agreed to climb the mountain and assess the condition of the plane by clearing the area where it lay.

They scheduled their trip to the site for March, before the monsoon season began. It was already early February, but surprisingly, their applications for visas were approved within two weeks.

The flight route would take them to Biak Island via Hawaii on Indonesia's Garuda Airlines where a shuttle flight would get them into Capur in Irian Jaya. Once in Capur they would need to select a team of qualified natives essential for clearing the area and for setting up campsites near the wreckage.

They were all anxious to get started— knowing little of what awaited them.

Twenty-Two

The weary travelers were relieved and excited as they touched down on Biak Island, and they barely noticed that they had made it through customs, which consisted of having their passport stamped. The flight to Capur took two hours. As they descended, they could see the dense forest covering the mountains. A chill came over Jill as they crossed over the fateful peak that rose five thousand feet above the valley floor.

Jill strained to see if she could catch a glimpse of the wreckage, but the jungle had long since completely swallowed it up. Each member of their party stared out the windows in silence, as vivid memories of the past raced through their minds. The pilot circled the airport before making his final approach. Little remained of the Air Force base they had once known. Only one small hangar was visible. There were no buildings—not even a Quonset hut! The natives had carried away anything of value shortly after the base was abandoned. With the exception of the runway, the area was overgrown with cuna grass. The closest village was a quarter of a mile away.

The passengers disembarked when the old DC-3 transport's engines whistled into a crackling silence. They stepped off the plane forty yards in front of the lone remaining hangar, just large enough to service two aircraft at a time. The small office inside was used for the air travel service, which was very sparse. The hangar was manned by a native girl who sat at a desk marked "Taxi."

The five weary travelers climbed into a beat up 1939 Packard, and with their baggage piled on their laps, headed toward a line of muddy craters that apparently was the road to the village. In the village they found lodgings in a tiny, filthy flat-topped building, which served as the local motel. Living conditions were deplorable, but to most of the natives, who were illiterate and living in squalor, the guest building represented the ultimate in luxury. Very little progress had been made since the war, and though the people were governed locally, the Indonesian government held military control over the provinces. Foreigners were eyed with suspicion, except for the few missionaries in the area who were treated with great respect. Don knew he had to make contact with the missionary in the village who would be able to hire the proper guide to help them get to the crash site.

Jill did not complain about the surroundings. However, when she and Don were alone, Don aired his opinion. "We have to get started soon. We don't want to spend anymore time in this God-forsaken hole than we have to."

Joe Bates verbalized his thoughts up front. "Looks like we have a real challenge ahead of us, fellas. I haven't seen anything like this since Jill and I tried to get away from our captors long ago."

"You haven't seen the worst of it yet. Wait till we start up that mountain," Jerry added.

The group made their way to a café just at the edge of the village. The only Western food was eggs and bacon and some very rank coffee. Don inquired as to where they could find the American missionary. The owner directed them to a school building down the street. There they found a sandy-haired minister directing native children into a classroom. Jeff Snyder greeted them with a warm welcome and seemed very interested in the group's mission. He had been in Capur for the past two years and was aware of the military plane's existence although he had never seen it. Don asked the Reverend if he could recommend a guide and some good workers. In return, they would give the Mission a sizeable donation. The Reverend graciously accepted.

Within a day, the group along with five strong, local natives prepared to initiate their climb. Don paid them each five American dollars per day, and supplies cost very little since they all agreed they could subsist on a few staples.

Making their way through the tall grass, Don thought about the young native boy, Zainal. He felt sorry for not having had a chance to thank him for saving his life. Perhaps now he would have time to search for him while he was in the province. Jill remembered how she had been carried through the cuna grass on a stretcher; the pain she had experienced, and the sniper attack. She squeezed Don's hand occasionally as they walked together.

Jerry complained, "Hasn't changed much. Same damn tall grass. Hotter than hell! Climbing this mountain is going to be a bitch!"

"It certainly couldn't be tougher than our trip down many years ago," Jordan predicted.

"You guys aren't very encouraging," Bates said laughingly.

"Don't sweat it Joe. If you can't make it, Jordan and I will carry you," Jerry jested.

After hours into the trek, they reached the waterfall where Don had nearly lost his life. They sat down, exhausted, and ate their lunch. The natives had done an excellent job of leading them thus far, laughing and chattering as they rested.

Moving again, the caravan moved more slowly and cautiously as the jungle grew denser. The towering ferns reached heights of nearly fifty feet, and they could barely see the sun through the jungle canopy. The steep inclines were difficult to manage, and the Americans were feeling their age as they tried to keep up with the young natives. The higher they climbed, the slower their pace. Everything they observed was enveloped in a gray mist and green walls. A mid-day shower drenched them, and then came the sweltering humidity.

After eight hours, the native's chatter became more stirring. The group climbed a steep gully, then up one last wall of mud and vines, and before them rested the P-61! The plane was on its belly with the nose pointed toward the top of the mountain—just short of the five thousand foot peak!

"Jesus, she hasn't moved an inch!" Jerry shouted.

Jordan gazed at the fallen war bird. "I'd say she has weathered the elements quite well."

They knew what they had to do. Don asked the native leader to clear the area for a campsite, as darkness would be on them soon. The natives quickly cleared the area. The men were anxious to inspect the aircraft more closely but decided to wait till daylight.

As night fell, a host of nocturnal noises erupted. Jill shuddered and moved closer to Don. She took comfort that he was with her, but she still felt a cold chill with each sound.

For the next few days, the team was able to stay in a hut that the natives had erected. The hut sheltered them from the tropical, torrential downpours and the pesky insects.

Assessing the disassembly of the craft was Don's major concern. Together they needed to make a list of the tools required to separate the wings from the fuselage and the engines from the wings.

Dismantling the craft in this manner would allow a helicopter to lift the plane out in sections. After an initial check, they discovered that the retracted main wheels still had air in their tires just as the missionary had reported!

The team checked and re-checked what was needed for their project. Tired and weatherworn, they made their descent, after being on the mountain four days. The trip down was more treacherous than they had imagined. Twice the guide encountered huge poisonous snakes along the trail. Slippery wet grass often caused team members to lose their footing.

After another six grueling hours, they arrived at the base of the mountain. Joe Bates contracted a high fever and had great difficulty keeping up with the others. The natives carried him through the tall grass to the village. He was treated by the mission doctor and was told to remain in bed for a couple of days.

Meanwhile, Don set out to find the tools needed for the dismantling. He contacted the pilot of the commuter airline that had brought them from Biak. Given the proper funds, the pilot said he could purchase the tools on his next flight to Biak. He said he would need three thousand dollars.

"Three thousand!" Don blurted out. "I don't have that kind of cash on me!"

"Do you carry a VISA card my friend?"

"Well, yes I do."

"That will work. VISA cards are accepted anywhere in Indonesia."

Don decided not to give the pilot his VISA card. Instead, he told him he would accompany him to Biak. The pilot booked them on the very next flight out in the afternoon. Jill stayed behind to look after Bates, while Jerry and Jordan accompanied Don to shop for the required tools and supplies.

Luckily, the pilot was familiar with where to take them for the things they needed. And once they were there, he even helped them negotiate the prices. Soon they were on their way back to Capur.

Jill was anxious to see them and explained that Joe's condition had worsened. At one point she thought he wasn't going to make it. "I'm really worried about him, Don. I think I should stay with him when you return to the crash site. How long do you think it will take to disassemble the plane?"

Don estimated it would take two days for the task, and Jill confirmed her decision to stay behind. The next morning they assembled their team and started up the steep slopes again with their heavy load of supplies. The extra weight of the tools added two hours to their climb.

Disassembling the twin boons from the wings was more difficult than they had expected. The head of one of the bolts holding a boon severed, and they had no way to get the bolt out except to cut it. Worst of all, it was a main spar bolt. Don feared this would be a major setback when they reassembled the craft back in the States, and he fretted over this for hours. Jerry consoled him saying, "We had to screw something up or else this wouldn't have been much fun."

"That's not much consolation Jerry. Do you realize how difficult it is going to be to reconstruct the main spar?"

"Hell, I don't know anything about that. But I'll bet you can do it once we get this baby home. What do you think Tuskegee?"

"Can't rightly say, but knowing Don, he'll find a way."

By the end of the day, they had disassembled the two tail boons from the wings and had both engines off the aircraft. They estimated they could finish their work before noon of the next day.

Surveying the large pieces of the aircraft, Don estimated the airlift requirements. "It's going to take five or ten lifts to get all of her off this mountain. We'll have to make a pad up here so a chopper can set down."

"Where do you propose we can get a chopper big enough to lift this bird?" Jordan asked.

"Haven't got a clue."

"It will cost a fortune when you find one," Jerry interjected, pessimistically.

The next morning the helicopter pad was completed. The team was ready to start back down the mountain. Before leaving, Don took pictures of the wreckage to show the section sizes that needed to be airlifted.

Within six hours they were back at the village and went directly to the Mission Church Hospital, where they found Jill sitting by herself.

"Don, Joe is in real danger. They don't seem to know what to do for him," she said in a worried tone.

"I'm sure they have treated hundreds of malaria cases like Joe's. They'll get to the bottom of it. Do you think we could go in and see him?"

"They asked me to let him rest. I came out here because I wanted to be nearby. If we ask the nurse maybe she will let us see him for a little while."

The nurse gave them permission for a short visit.

Joe was on oxygen. His face was pale white, and his eyes were closed. When Joe heard their voices, he motioned with his hand that he was okay.

While they were standing there, the doctor came in and stated, "His fever has broken and he will be all right by morning. After a good night's rest, he should be ready to be released." Relieved, they clasped Joe's hand and bid him goodnight. Outside, Don said, "You did a wonderful job honey. I knew we could count on you."

Joe was discharged the following day well enough to make the homeward trip, all the while insisting he would come back to help with the recovery.

"I need to do one more thing before I leave Capur," Don said to Jill. "I'd like to find the boy who saved my life. I believe I should start at the mission."

When they met with Rev. Snyder, Don started by thanking him for his help during their stay. They felt they had made a life-long friend.

"Rev. when I was here during the war, a young Dani boy saved my life. He disappeared into the jungle before I could thank him properly. Do you know how I might find him? His name was Zainal."

"I'll check through my school records. Every student's name is here since the school was started." In a short time Rev. Snyder looked up with a smile on his face.

"The only Zainal I have listed was from the Dani tribe. He went through our school in 1946, graduated and went to Jakarta to further his education. His full name is Zainal Sudar."

"It has to be him! Once I get back to the States, I'll try contacting the University of Jakarta. Maybe they can tell me how to reach him. I'm so grateful to you Reverend. I'll try to keep in touch with you once we get back home. Good-bye friend." Jill kissed his cheek as they departed.

Upon returning to the States, Don put his thoughts of Zainal aside and threw himself into researching the P-61's wing construction. He had to find out how he could reconstruct the damaged wing spar when the time came. He was astonished to learn that of the 760 night fighters produced during the war, only four now remained, three of which were "C" models. They were attempting to recover the only "B" combat model in existence! If successful in their recovery and reconstruction, they would have the only P-61 Black Widow night fighter left flying in the world!

Twenty-Three

With the revelation of the rarity of the P-61, Don began to worry. He suspected that if word were to get out, some Warbird collectors might rush to obtain recovery rights, and wealthier ones could pay whatever was needed to swipe the aircraft out from under him. Don quickly set up a conference call with Jerry, Jordan and Joe, outlined his concerns and swore them to secrecy. All three agreed wholeheartedly and urged him to act swiftly with the Indonesian authorities in getting full rights to the wreckage.

Don and Jill set out for the Indonesian Embassy in Washington, D.C., to make the claim the P-61 wreckage was American property, lost in the liberation of New Guinea. The Embassy was a beautiful old mansion on famed "Embassy Row" in what was once the home of a prominent Washington socialite and owner of the world's largest gemstone, "The Hope Diamond." Jill was impressed with the mansion and her eyes surveyed the surroundings with keen interest. Don, on the other hand, cast his eyes immediately upon the Embassy Directory.

The first office he saw printed on the list was that of the Air Attaché. His eyes stopped abruptly when he saw the name of a Colonel Zainal Sudar!

"Jill, look at this name!" Don said, pointing to the gold-lettered inscription.

"Good Lord, Don, do you think there is any connection?"

"Stranger things have happened. This is where we should start."

Don's heart was beating faster as they exited the elevator at the second floor. Directly in front of them was the "Office of the Air Attaché." The receptionist greeted them politely and asked if they had an appointment.

"I'm sorry to say we haven't, Mam. But we have the feeling that the Colonel would want to see us. So if you would please tell him it is important that we see him and that we've traveled a long way to be here, we'd appreciate it," Don appealed.

"I'll talk to him and see if it might be possible, but he does have a very busy schedule at the moment," she responded.

Soon an inner office door opened and a smartly uniformed Indonesian Air Force Officer emerged. He was a handsome man of medium build and a light brown complexion. Don studied his facial features. He was trying to conjure up an image of the young tribesman who had befriended him. The round face and sparkling eyes matched those of the young boy he once knew.

"How do you do? I'm Colonel Sudar. How may I be of assistance?"

"Colonel, I believe we have met before. Perhaps you don't remember me, but I've never forgotten you."

"I don't think I recall exactly. Have you ever been in my country?"

"Yes, during World War II. I was stationed at an airbase in Capur. I was a pilot with the United States Army Air Corps. I fell from a waterfall, and a wonderful young man came from out of nowhere and saved my life. You were a very young man then. My name is Don Jennings."

"Yes, yes now I recall. I didn't know your name but you were badly injured. You had crashed on the mountain just above the airbase. When you fell down the waterfall, I helped you down the mountain!"

"Then you are Zainal! What a strange coincidence that I should find you here! When I saw your name in the directory, I just had to know if you were the same man that saved my life!"

"What a small place the world really is," Zainal replied enthusiastically.

"Colonel, this is my wife Jill. You saved her life too!"

"I wasn't aware that I did that—how so?"

"Jill was also aboard my aircraft when I crashed on that mountain. By finding me and getting me to safety and to help, a rescue team was able to climb the mountain and bring down the others."

"I didn't know there were others involved in the crash."

"Well, for some reason, you left us as soon as you had found help for me. I never had a chance to thank you for what you did."

"I believed my work was done and I needed to get back to my village. My parents would have really been worried if I hadn't returned before sundown."

"I'm curious now. How did you get into the Indonesian Air Force?"

"I guess I have you to thank for that. You see, after I returned to my village, I thought about you many times. I thought about how courageous you were. I admired you and wanted to fly those great birds like you did. It was a long process. First I attended the Mission School at Capur. After graduation, the missionary encouraged me to go to Jakarta for more study. When the war with the Dutch was over and Indonesia got her independence, I worked my way through college in Jakarta. Then I joined the Air Force."

"That's incredible! And you became a flying officer?" Jill asked.

"Yes, I'm rated in about every airplane we have and wound up my flying career as a fighter command pilot. When I was promoted to Colonel they made me an Air Attaché, since I could speak

English, French and German. I've served in England and France before coming to the United States."

"Colonel Sudar," Jill began.

"Oh please call me Zainal."

"May I suggest we have lunch together and celebrate this glorious reunion? I know you two have a lot to talk about."

"I'd be honored, Mrs. Jennings. I'll cancel my other appointments and join you in a minute," Zainal replied in a gentlemanly manner.

Zainal took the pair to lunch at an Indonesian restaurant just a few blocks away. During lunch Don disclosed his reasons for seeking the help of the Embassy. Zainal listened intently as he smoked his clove cigarettes.

"I understand your urgency, Don. But I must warn you, our government is slow to act on outside requests for recovery of World War II relics. We have so many war relics in all parts of our country; a country that is made up of over 3,000 islands. However, the United States has been a good friend to us. They liberated us from the Japanese. And they supported our quest for independence from the Dutch. Let me see what I can do. My government will most likely want something in exchange for the wreckage of your aircraft. Our history shows we have been subjected to outside forces and foreign exploitation for many years. Now that we have achieved independence, the people are eager to regain and retain what they believe is rightfully theirs. So it is a question of economics. Do you see what I mean?"

"Yes I do Zainal. What do you think they might want in exchange?"

"That would have to be determined by the Minister of Trade."

"Would you be able to process our request?"

"I would be happy to try to expedite this to the limited extent that I can. First I will talk with the Air Marshall in Jakarta. Please be patient though; they will take their time in responding. However, I can give you the rights of recovery of the wreckage today. This action will protect the aircraft for your project. We can work out the actual recovery agreement when you find out what our government wants in exchange."

"That is just wonderful; thank you so much— I never expected to move this far today."

Zainal's broad smile was his friendly sign that a pact had been set in place between the two of them. After lunch, Zainal took Don and Jill to meet his family and to tour his home. Zainal's graciousness, personal attention and sincerity was obviously heartfelt and was emotionally moving to Don.

Within two weeks, Zainal called to say a retired Air Marshal of the Indonesian Air Force had to be consulted on the request. This man was given permission to negotiate the exchange of the wreckage. Payment would be the exchange of a flyable WWII Primary Trainer known as the Ryan PT-22 for the downed P-61 Black Widow night fighter. The Indonesian government wants the trainer for their Air Force Museum.

The news panicked Don. He had no idea where to find the Ryan PT-22 or how much it would cost. However, without delay, he called Zainal and said he would meet their offer. Upon his arrival home, Don picked up a copy of "Trade-a-Plane," a national monthly publication. No PT-22's were available. Don called Jerry, Jordan and Joe to ask for their input and help.

A month later Jerry had located a PT-22 in the backyard of an aircraft mechanic's home in San Diego. It needed work but Jerry felt it was in great shape. The next morning, Don and Jill were on their way to San Diego. Jerry joined them in La Jolla and by noon they were knocking on the owner's door.

The man showed great pride in his treasure. He had purchased the plane at an Army Surplus sale thirty years ago and had been trying to get it into flying condition ever since. He showed them sales slips for repair expenses so far, which totaled several thousand dollars.

"I hate to sell her, but my wife developed multiple sclerosis, a crippling disease. I can't spend the money or the time on the plane anymore, and I need money now for my wife's treatments. I'm asking $35,000 for the plane."

"What other repairs does it need to make it airworthy?" Don asked.

"All she needs is a motor tune-up. Come out back and you can take a look at her."

The plane was sitting near the man's garage. The silver luster of the all-metal, low-wing craft, glimmered in the sunlight. The Ryan PT-22 was flown by Don's upper classmen at Ryan Field where he had taken primary flight training. He and his lower classmen jokingly referred to the plane as the "May Tag Messerschmidt," believing the older Stearman PT-17 bi-plane they flew was a much better airplane.

Don could see that the owner had restored the plane beautifully. The only glitch was the price. Don stroked the skin of the aircraft's wing and said, "I can't deny she's a rare beauty. You've done a good job on her. Would you take a certified check for $23,000?"

The man rubbed his chin and then replied firmly, "No, but I'll take $27,000 and have her 'purring like a kitten' before you take her away."

Don glanced at Jill and Jerry. They showed no reaction. "Got yourself a deal! When can you have her ready to fly?" Don shot back.

"Give me a week, and you can haul her to the nearest airport and fly her away!" Don shook the kindly old man's hand and assured him he'd be back as soon as the week was up.

Don felt a little guilty over having the owner lower the price under the circumstances. But Jerry and Jill assured him that the man had gotten the price he really wanted.

True to his word, the owner of the craft called Don at the end of the week to report the vintage trainer was ready to fly. Arrangements were made to transport the plane to Lindbergh Field in San Diego, where they could fly it out. Don and Jill were at the field when the craft arrived. A flight instructor, familiar with the trainer, took Don up for a check flight and Don mastered the controls in short order.

Jill had never flown in an open cockpit airplane. She loved the feel of the sun and wind in her face. Don could see how delighted she was with the experience as he watched her smiling face in his rear view mirror. He climbed to six thousand feet then told Jill to make sure her safety belt was tight. Then he put the craft into a slow roll. He reduced power and pointed the nose downward. As the craft picked up air speed, he eased back on the control stick. He started a steep climb, added full throttle and did a full loop. Pulling out at the bottom of the loop, Don could see Jill smiling. She was thoroughly enjoying the ride, and Don was falling in love with this marvelous little plane. So much so, that he hated the thought of having to give it up. "Oh, open cockpit flying, there isn't anything like it," he told himself as he danced through white puffy clouds all the way back to Ryan Field in Hemet.

When they landed, Don put the airplane in a rented hangar and headed for home to call Zainal to tell him of their purchase. Zainal was delighted to learn of their success and said he would arrange for the former Air Marshall of Indonesia to come out to see the plane.

Air Marshall Wisnu was a pleasant man and spoke fluent English. He himself had flown PT-22's as an Indonesian Air Cadet. He informed them he had trained under US Air Force instructors at a base near Bakersfield, California in 1946. Zainal and

Marshall Wisnu inspected the aircraft meticulously, and the Marshall finally smiled approvingly. Don felt like he had just sold his favorite puppy.

Twenty-Four

*W*ith the recovery rights to the P-61 wreckage now assured, Don was faced with the next hurdle—where to get a helicopter big enough to lift the plane off the mountain. He posed the question to Colonel Zainal. Zainal advised him to seek Marshall Wisnu's help and offered to facilitate a meeting. Unfortunately they learned the Marshall had already left the country.

Undaunted, Don decided to seek his District Congressman's help. The Congressman was impressed with Don's story and seemed interested. As a member of the Armed Services Committee, the Congressman had knowledge of the Air Force's huge C5A Transports training flights in and out of

Guam and frequent flights back to the States. He promised to ask Air Force officials if they would pick up the wreckage on one of their return trips. Don was elated. But a week later his hopes faded quickly…the Congressman called to say his request was denied because the recovery project was a private venture.

Don's spirits were at low ebb when he received an unexpected formal invitation from the Indonesian Ambassador himself to attend a gala at the Embassy. Don immediately phoned Colonel Zainal to see if Zainal was aware of the invitation. Zainal confessed happily that he did know of the invitation, and in fact he had helped to formulate the announcement list. He believed it would give Don the opportunity to talk personally to the Ambassador about his recovery project. Spirits renewed, Don added Jill's name to the RSVP and promptly returned it.

Their arrival at the Embassy was exciting and accompanied by feelings of anticipation and expectation. This level of pomp and circumstance was new to both Don and Jill and they were impressed with the number of dignitaries attending the social. It was obvious to both of them that Zainal had purposefully chosen this opportune time for Don to do some public relations work for the project.

Zainal introduced Don to the Ambassador and suggested that Don bring the Ambassador "up to speed" on his recovery efforts and the exchange agreement he had made with the former Indonesian

Air Marshall. To Don's surprise, the Ambassador listened attentively, rubbed his chin, smiled and responded. "Mr. Jennings, there is a man here tonight who may be of some assistance to you. Come, I'll introduce you to him. You fill him in on your story about the P-61 and of what you need to complete the exchange."

Don followed the kindly diplomat across the crowded ballroom where he met George Baron, an American public relations consultant to the Ambassador.

"I'll leave you two and get back to my other guests. You tell Mr. Baron the story."

"What's on your mind, Mr. Jennings?" Baron asked.

"Mr. Baron, I have a real problem. The Ambassador thinks you can help me," Don began as he outlined his project and the requirements that had turned into his dilemma.

"Sounds like a job for a big helicopter, Mr. Jennings."

"I'm afraid it is and there aren't any choppers capable for the air-lift in Irian Jaya."

"I do a lot of public relations work for Indonesia. My first impression is you need the Indonesian military's support, since the former Air Marshall wants your P-22 for their museum," Baron advised.

"I agree Mr. Baron. But how do I go about convincing them to help?"

"Looks as though you've already received approval for the exchange by the Air Marshall. You need a little push from my friend, the Minister of Culture in Indonesia."

"Is he in the States?"

"At the moment he's in China. I'm flying to Bejing tomorrow and I'll see him early this week. I'll speak to him of your progress thus far with the Indonesian Air Attaché and Marshal Wisnu. In working with these people for several years, I've found they move rather slowly until you've reached the right person to deal with. I can see you've got the Ambassador's support on your project and now we have to work through their system. Let me see if I can get the Minister of Culture moving on this, Mr. Jennings. I promise I'll be in touch through Colonel Zainal as soon as possible."

"I'd certainly appreciate anything you can do Mr. Baron, and I thank you so much for your interest," Don replied hopefully.

Don and Jill enjoyed the rest of the evening mingling with the high society guests, and they returned to their hotel relaxed and convinced that Zainal had not only pointed them in the right direction but had given them the opportunity to put the connections and mechanisms in place for accomplishing the end task in Irian Jaya. Their hunch was right. A week later Zainal phoned to say the Minister of Culture had arranged for the major oil company in Indonesia to assist in the recovery. Additionally, they promised to ship the plane by freighter to Long Beach if Jennings and his recovery team crated the individual sections when the lift was completed.

With this news, Don notified Jerry, Jordan and Joe to pack their bags in preparation for their final recovery mission. Hastily, they regrouped and returned to Capur. As soon as they arrived, Don prevailed upon their missionary friend, Rev. Snyder, to recruit carpenters for the crating job. And this was none too soon, as three days later a huge military helicopter arrived from Jakarta, three thousand miles away.

To the team's delight, the chopper deposited them at the crash site sparing them the long trudge up the mountainside. After several hours of grueling work, the team had the wreckage off the mountain.

Though tired and weary from the rigorous ordeal, Don knew their work was not finished. They immediately began to direct and to supervise the native crating job and the handling processes needed to get the crates aboard the waiting ocean freighter. Once all of that was done the exhausted team rested for a day then headed for home to await the arrival of their prize.

As soon as they returned home they were faced with finding a suitable facility in which to conduct the restoration work. Fortune struck again and Don located an empty hangar at a private airport near his home. The rental was inexpensive. Moreover, this area of California was one with several large aircraft production factories and provided a mecca for recruiting men with aircraft assembly experience. And by the time the cargo transport arrived with the airplane, the group had prepared the exchange aircraft, the PT-22, for loading on the freighter at Long Beach Harbor.

Finances were running very low for the group at this stage of the project. They had to find a way to get substantial additional funding for the restoration. Don struck on an idea. He had photographed every phase of the recovery and believed he could sell his photos and story to a national magazine and he set about trying to sell a photo journal article. Weeks went by before a major magazine offered him a publishing contract, and the contract specified that upon completion of the restoration, the magazine would receive any funds generated from the plane's air-show appearances for one year. Don agreed with the proposal with the one exception that he wanted any private donations for the project during the same one-year time frame they had proposed. The magazine accepted his counter offer.

When the first pictorials and feature story were released, Don was besieged with phone calls and letters offering contributions. Dozens of volunteers offered their help with the project. Many of them were former aircraft engineers and skilled aircraft workers at Northrop where the P-61s were produced.

Don was overwhelmed with the response and overloaded with paper work. Jill and Lillian agreed to handle the correspondence in securing a crack restoration team. To enhance the sponsoring magazines' feature stories, Don photographed every step of the restoration phase, submitting each on a timely basis to keep the project moving along. Don found himself married to his work—often working twelve hours a day, obsessed with completing the restoration ahead of their projected schedule and before their contractual agreement with the magazine ran out. The magazine editors were pleased with the progress and agreed to run the articles more frequently as the work neared completion. After each magazine release, requests from the media for interviews flowed in. Don was delighted with this attention but it added more time to his already busy schedule. Finally he decided to stop further media coverage until they could announce plans for the actual maiden flight. The timing would coincide with the 25th anniversary of the plane's initial test flight during WWII. And just six months later, the shiny black fighter, restored to perfection, was officially certified by the Federal Aviation Authority inspectors as air-worthy.

One morning before dawn, Don climbed into the once so familiar cockpit, started the engines and taxied into take-off position. Holding firmly on the brakes, he ran up the engines to full throttle and checked his magnetos. Satisfied that he had done his pre-flight check thoroughly, he advanced the throttles and roared down the runway. The plane lifted gracefully into the sky—shattering the silence of the still, thin air. In minutes he was high over the glow of city lights below. At five thousand feet he leveled off, trimmed the aircraft for cruising speed and did a series of banking turns. He pulled the nose upward until he approached stall speed. The aircraft responded perfectly throughout the maneuvers.

Satisfied with its performance, he headed back to the field. The group had waited anxiously for his return. They ran out to welcome him as he climbed down from the plane. Jill rushed into his arms.

"What do you think?" She questioned excitedly.

"Couldn't be more pleased! She performed better than the first day I flew her in 1945. I just have one complaint. You guys weren't aboard."

"Did you try the radar scope?" Jerry asked.

"No, I didn't. I thought I'd leave that up to my radar operator on our next flight."

"And when will that be?" Jerry asked— hardly able to contain himself.

"Let's see. The sun comes up in about an hour. How would that suit your schedule?"

"I'm ready. How about our observers going along to make it official?" Jerry said laughingly.

"That would be perfect, and since there are no Air Force crew restrictions, we'll work out the seating arrangements to suit ourselves," Don said jokingly and all joined in a hardy belly laugh.

Jordan and Joe congratulated Don on his test flight. Joe placed his hand on the nose of the plane and suggested that they give it a name and have some nose art painted on too.

"Anyone have a suggestion as to what we should call her?" Joe asked.

They all fell silent for a moment. Jill then shouted out, "Unforgettable Lady!" They all agreed it was most appropriate and adopted the name instantly.

"How about we paint an attractive lady like Jill, wearing a red dress and carrying an American flag on the nose?" Jerry blurted out.

"No argument from me on that," Joe fired back.

"Are you sure you'd like that?" Jill said shyly.

"Honey," Don shouted out. "We couldn't be more sure!" The art work was begun the next day and when completed the nose of the beautiful black fighter featured the name "Unforgettable Lady" in white below a well-proportioned young lady wearing a red dress with an American flag in hand. Painted in gray and near the rear of the cockpit window was a listing of the crew—Brigadier General Joe Bates, Squadron Commander, 1st Lt. Don Jennings, Aircraft Commander, 1st Lt. Jerry Hurwitz, Radar Operator, Crew: Colonel Jordan (Tuskegee) Bond and Sergeant Jill Harris.

Don informed the magazine that they were ready for a formal christening and public showing of the P-61. When the day arrived more than six news services were on hand. The media hailed the event as a miracle resurrection of a World War II Night Fighter found in the jungles of New Guinea. The plane was soon in demand at annual air shows throughout the country. The magazine was delighted now that they were at last getting handsome returns on their investment. They began their air show schedules on the west coast. Both Jordan and Joe had kept their commercial pilot ratings current, so they could alternate with Don in flying the P-61 to the air show performances. The wives were content to pass out literature and talk with visitors who flocked to get close to the aircraft. They wound up their show commitments at Oshkosh, Wisconsin where upwards of 250, 000 visitors attended daily at the five-day event. "Unforgettable Lady" had become a household word among air show promoters across the country.

Satisfied that they had accomplished their goal, the group decided it was time to find the plane a permanent home. They contacted officials of the Air Force Museum in Dayton, Ohio and offered to donate the plane for static display. The Museum accepted the offer and scheduled a crew to fly the plane to Dayton.

On the morning of October 10, 1997, Don, Jerry and Joe Bates landed at Marsh Field. Jordan and Jill met them. Grouped together, they stood proudly at attention as a color guard approached, led by the field's Adjutant General. In a brief ceremony, entitlement to the aircraft was turned over to the U.S. Air Force.

The group joined hands and watched an Air Force pilot and two crewmembers board the plane. They continued their vigil in silence until the plane left the ground and disappeared in the distance.

On October 11, 1997 a front page story in the Times Report read:

Three Men Survive Crash of
Rare World War II Plane

Denver: Three U.S. Air Force crewmen survived the crash of the famed World War II P-61 Black Widow night fighter "Unforgettable Lady" near here late yesterday. The plane was totally destroyed.

The pilot, a WWII veteran, had flown over 3,000 hours in this same type of aircraft during the war. The craft was being ferried to the Air Force Museum in Dayton, Ohio. Eyewitnesses reported the plane was climbing steeply away from the airport when suddenly it "shuttered and hung in mid-air like a fluttering kite." The aircraft nosed over and spun downward. Witnesses reported seeing three parachutes deploy before the aircraft disappeared behind a row of trees north of the airport.

Acknowledgments

First and foremost, I am indebted to my fiancée,
Anne E. Barner for her support, inspiration and
tireless work in the preparation of my manuscript.
I could not have done it without you!

I am grateful to my nephew, James W. Meade
for his editorial expertise, suggestions
and motivation to finalize this novel.

Thanks to Peter Stevenson for
his editorial support as well.

A special thanks to Tuskegee Airman,
Dr. Eugene Richardson for providing his
photo for the cover of this book.

Finally, I thank my family; Dawn Woolf,
Abbey Naugle, Addam Woolf, Tom Remsnyder,
Ted Canaday, Jeannine Marttila and special friends,
Chrissy Baerwald and Bridget Palecek
for urging me to publish this story.

About The Author

Orin F. Remsnyder has been in love with airplanes ever since he ventured into the wild blue with a barnstorming pilot at the age of seven.

As a teenager, he worked in the aviation industry before making his first solo flight in 1942 at Niagara Falls, N.Y. At age nineteen he joined the US Army Air Corps and served three years.

He graduated from the National Academy of Broadcasting and Juniata College. In his diverse career, the author worked in press and radio; served fifteen years as a church minister; taught public school and held executive administration posts for two national community public education associations. Lastly he served as Executive Vice President of the Mid-Atlantic Air Museum in Reading, Pennsylvania.

As a member of the Silver Wings Fraternity, Orin flew privately for nearly fifty years before hanging up his goggles in 1992. He is a proud father, grandfather and a great grandfather. He now resides in Harrisburg, Pa, and enjoys writing, traveling, playing the piano and golfing.